A prequel to

The Chains Trilogy

The

Retrieval

A novella by

Rob Cherville

ISBN-13: 978-1508968757
ISBN-10: 1508968756

Published by
Aullton House Books, Derbyshire UK

Printed by
CreateSpace, Charleston SC

robcherville@aulltonhouse.org.uk

For my wife and my daughters
with thanks for all their loving support and
encouragement.

And for my readers
whose interest and good will continues to inspire me.

Preface

Some readers of my previous book "Breaking Chains" have expressed curiosity about events referred to, but not fully explained, in that story.

It is clearly understood that, some two years or more prior to the opening of "Breaking Chains", Abby Montrayne was kidnapped. It is also clear that a young man named Richard figured somehow as the initiator of those events. However, where he came from is a mystery, and how he inserted himself into the Montrayne family circle is unexplained. Readers are in no doubt that Abby was traumatized by what occurred, but they are left wondering why she was kidnapped, what exactly happened to her and to what lengths did her father have to go in order to recover her.

What follows is an attempt to satisfy that curiosity. Initially developing as an idea for a short story, the project soon began to exceed the bounds of that genre. In its final form, perhaps it should more rightly be described as a novella. In whatever way you, my reader, choose to view the telling of this brief episode, my hope is that curiosity will have been satisfied and that you will have enjoyed travelling the journey to the retrieval.

Rob Cherville

South Derbyshire, UK
February 2015

Wednesday

23rd April 2003

Market Place, Uttoxeter – 8:35 am

When it came to computers and the internet, Richard Bancroft knew he was up there with the best. Determined always to push the boundaries of what was possible, he had just experienced a fruitful few days set free, by the Easter holidays, from the usual constraints of work and study. Returning once again to his normal routine, he was sure – well, reasonably sure – that none of his recent activities would come back to bite him.

Seated now at his regular workbench in the back room of the computer shop, his favourite micro-screwdriver hovering over the revealed innards of a dead laptop, Richard smiled to himself. He loved everything about computers. Chips and processors, RAM and ROM, hardware, software, firmware were all nourishment to his lonely soul. They were logical, impassive and undemanding, never arguing back or creating situations that he was emotionally unable to deal with.

The slender fingers of his left hand moved to adjust the angle of the work lamp on his desk and, as he leant forward, long tendrils of dark hair drifted down in front of his eyes. It would have made sense to restrain his generous locks in a ponytail while working, they were certainly long enough, but he couldn't bring himself to adopt such a girlish hairstyle. Peering closely at the tiny screws which needed to be removed, he nodded slowly. As always, he had supreme confidence in his ability to release the potential hidden in the complex circuitry beneath his fingers.

He had every right to be confident.

He had an IT degree under his belt and was well on his way to an MSc in Internet Web Technologies. Tim Wells, the owner of Byte Store Networks, considered himself fortunate to have Richard on his staff, even though the young man seemed strangely quiet and introverted and his studies meant that the position could only be part-time. Before closing for the Easter holiday, the pair of them had agreed that they would both come in early on the first day back after the extended break. They needed to start making inroads on repairs that would have lain untouched for several days.

5

A loud knocking on the front door of the computer repair shop caught Richard's attention. He looked up, frowning.

"I'll get it," said Tim, turning away from the motherboard he'd been working on. "Can't think who it's going to be at this time."

An early customer, perhaps, who was impatient to get to work and couldn't read the opening times posted on the door.

But then customers usually knocked politely, and this banging was rather more insistent. The door quivered under a renewed onslaught causing the internal warning bell to jangle imperiously.

Richard lowered his screwdriver and twisted in his chair to peer through the doorway between the workshop and the sales area at the front of the store. Tim's back disappeared as he sidled around the counter to get to the door. At that moment, Richard had a clear view of the two men standing outside the shop, and his heart lurched as a cold nausea settled in his stomach.

Black eyes stared out of a wide-browed, Slavic face with an intensity that might drill holes through the glass panels of the door. If drilling failed, this tall guy's broad shoulders could certainly smash it in if the need arose.

You don't forget a face like that, and Richard knew where he'd seen it before. He also knew what they'd come for.

And, therefore, he knew that the dung-heap now threatening to engulf him was as deep as it gets.

He snatched up his red backpack from under his workbench and headed for the rear door and the alleyway to safety.

Simpkins Logistics, Uttoxeter – 9.10 am

Mykyta Shwetz turned his head slowly to fix his dark eyes on the black, ceramic throwing knife that quivered in the wooden doorframe only millimetres from his right ear.

Bohdan Simonenko also stared at it. His elegantly manicured fingers had barely twitched as they launched the lethal dart on its fifteen foot journey across his office to land exactly

6

where he had intended. There was no satisfaction in his eyes; no hint of pleasure in the skill he had just demonstrated. It was what it was, a talent honed to such a high level of precision that he simply took it for granted that the knife would pierce whatever he wished. Sometimes it was a warning, as now, but at other times its short flight had ended in lethal finality.

"I…want…it…back," said Simonenko in the guttural Ukrainian of his motherland. He might have changed his name to Danny Simpkins, but he still thought in his native tongue. "No excuse… … No failure……Bring me that hard drive… … and dispose of the boy."

Shwetz had the powerful physique of a weightlifter and the black, expressionless eyes of a lizard. No-one encountering him in a bar would ever dream of jostling his drink. There were very few people in the world that he was afraid of, but this tall man in his stylish, hand-tailored suit was one of the few. Shwetz might not have the needle-sharp intellect of his boss, but he was far from stupid, which was why Simonenko trusted him to manage this branch of his highly successful haulage business when matters required his own absence.

But that was before Shwetz had made this gravest of errors.

He had tried to retrieve his mistake but, as he had just explained to Simonenko, the boy had not been at the computer repair shop when he had called there less than an hour ago. The owner of the shop had obviously been surprised to find the workroom empty when he had shown them in. Shwetz had believed him when he had said that Richard had been working in the back room only a moment or two beforehand, and he couldn't imagine where the boy had got to. His amazement had seemed so genuine that Shwetz had been sure he was telling the truth. Changing tack, he had asked for the return of the faulty hard drive which the young man had mistakenly removed from the office of Simpkins Logistics when he had been called in to repair their computer system before the long Easter weekend.

And that's when things had become awkward.

In the back room of Byte Store Networks stood a large, black, plastic bin of the sort regularly used for trash in areas where they hadn't yet been replaced by a wheelie-bin. This was where Tim and Richard tossed defunct components which were incapable of being repaired. Periodically, the collected items were removed and taken for recycling.

That morning it had been completely empty, and Tim explained that Richard had dealt with the recycling before the shop had closed for the holiday. He had been most apologetic, suggesting to his surly customer that the drive was probably even then in a container of similarly useless components on its way to China for disposal.

To Shwetz and his companion, this had all sounded entirely plausible, and both were reluctant to raise suspicion by turning what should have seemed only a minor issue into something of more significance. Faced with this brick wall, Shwetz had not the faintest idea what Simonenko would want him to do next, so he and his companion had left the shop to convey the bad news to their boss back at the haulage depot.

The journey might only have taken twelve minutes, but Shwetz had spent every moment of the drive sweating with fear. With the twenty-twenty vision of hindsight, he knew he should never have taken it upon himself to call in a local computer specialist when their company IT system had failed. He tried to convince himself that he could not be blamed for the fact that the problem had occurred at a time when Simonenko had been away massaging contacts in Latvia. Nor, he thought, had it been his fault that the company's resident IT expert, Marko Balanchuk, had been missing – presumed arrested or, more likely, dead – somewhere in Moldova.

But he knew his boss and, therefore, he knew exactly where the blame was going to fall. He also knew the penalty for failure.

Drawing his eyes away from the knife, Shwetz turned to face his boss.

"You do not believe that the drive is lost?" he said slowly, half statement, half question.

Simonenko made an effort to rein in his temper. Shwetz was not a bad lieutenant; just lacking in imagination.

"This Bancroft did not take that hard drive for no good reason. He did not take it just to throw it in the trash. He will try to see what is on it."

Shwetz still didn't quite see the problem.

"But all the files that could harm us are encrypted," he said. "Even if the boy knows how to get at them, he still can't read them."

"He might," replied Simonenko. "There are young men… … and women… … whose brains are bigger and work much faster than yours. They understand these things, perhaps even better than Balanchuk, and they would think of our hard drive as… … er… … as a puzzle. And they would dig, and dig, and dig until they solve it."

Shwetz's heart was pounding and he tried to calm it by taking slow, deep breaths. Until that moment, he hadn't fully realised the enormity of his blunder.

"I will find the boy," he said, at last. "And I will make him tell me what he has done with the drive."

"And then you will dispose of him," added Simonenko.

Shwetz almost sighed with relief at this apparent reprieve.

"And then I will dispose of him."

Bramshall Road Park, Uttoxeter – 11.05 am

Richard sat with his back against an old, gnarled oak and rocked gently to and fro. The grass under the trees was still slightly damp with dew and moisture was beginning to soak through the heavy denim of his jeans. Even when the cold dampness reached his skin he didn't notice. His knees were drawn up tight to his chest, the soles of his trainers flat on the ground, his arms wrapped around his legs. His mind was whirling, trying to make sense of the little he knew. A train flashed past on the other side of the Picknall Brook, but he neither saw nor heard it.

He simply rocked; slowly, rhythmically, just as he always did when the stress of living became too much to handle. He knew he was different. He knew other young men didn't behave like this, but he couldn't help it. His parents had understood and had protected him from the worst assaults of an ill-informed public. As he had developed into his teen years, they had taught him how to adapt to the expectations of staff and pupils at school, so that he no longer stood out as being markedly different. He had learned how to respond to others, even to hold a conversation of sorts, not because he wanted to please them, but as a kind of self-defence. Understandably, he never made any friends and was always glad when the time came to retreat to the security of home.

Home was where he could find comfort in the solitude of the IT jungle that he called his bedroom – until that security had been snatched away by the tragedy of a motorway accident in which both parents had died. Orphaned and under-age, he had gone to live with his grandmother in the village of Newton-under-Grangewood.

The death of his parents had seemed to trip some kind of emotional switch in his brain. He had never really wanted to please anybody, but now they were no longer there, he wanted desperately to please his mum and dad. The way to do that was to put into practice every single thing they had tried to teach him. And in that he now excelled, just as he always did at anything he truly set his mind to.

For three years, university had become home. He still had no need of friends, but he had learnt how to get along. Some called him a geek – a few even called him that weird geek – but no-one denied his brilliance when it came to information technology. Maybe one day he'd make his name in the growing market for internet security. In the meantime he'd been honing his skills on a range of government networks, both at home and abroad, and he'd been amazed to discover just how lax government security could be.

He was still a student, post-graduate now, and home was a downstairs flat in a converted semi-detached house in Holly

Road, about half a mile away from where he sat and rocked in the park. The location of home might change but, with his familiar computers around him, it was always a place where he felt safe.

But not today, because home was where those people could find him.

And he mustn't be found, because he had discovered their secrets.

This time, he knew, he had gone too far.

Market Place, Uttoxeter – 1:35 pm

It was Abby's fault that they were there when it happened.

She and her father, James Montrayne, were making the most of the school holidays. She laughed as she skipped along the pavement, holding tightly to his hand, as six-year-olds are happy to do. He glanced down at her, smiling at her carefree dependence, and knowing that it wouldn't last. One day, all too soon, she'd be a teenager, pushing the boundaries as she struggled through puberty and adolescence. Would it be a struggle? It certainly had been for his younger sister, Jessica, who had developed the knack of straining boundaries to their absolute limits. He envisaged a rocky road ahead as he embraced the unfamiliar role of father to a girl emerging into womanhood.

Still, the training and experience that came with his line of work did offer some preparation for what lay ahead. No-one knew of anyone in his family, back through all the generations to the Conqueror, who had chosen employment as a school-teacher. Not, that is, until James Montrayne had made that decision on retiring as a major from the Royal Marines shortly after the death of his wife. He had ignored his father's protests and opted to emulate his dear Sarah's choice of profession. The reason was simple. He wanted to be on hand to care for his baby daughter. He also hadn't wanted to run the risk of Abby losing a second parent. His father, of course, had been most unhappy, and he let it be known. Teaching, especially primary school teaching, was not in his view an occupation worthy of the nephew of the twelfth Marquess of Thurvaston. James, however, had stood his ground.

As the second son of a second son, with little in the way of inheritance coming his way, he would do what he needed to do, and on his own terms.

He needn't have worried. His godmother, Lady Helena Marchmont, had discovered her soulmate to be a highly successful entrepreneur industrialist who subsequently turned out, to her great disappointment, to be impotent. Not having the inclination of her forebears to rectify this deficiency between sheets other than her husband's, she focussed her motherly love and attention on her only godchild. Surviving her husband, and with no children to inherit her significant wealth, she had chosen to bestow it on James Montrayne, her recently bereaved godson. With a young baby to rear, and no fortune of his own, she had reckoned he might be in need of hers.

Sadly, or fortunately, depending on your point of view, James had not remained a second son. Barely three weeks before Easter, a twin-engined Aerostar 700 had ploughed into a Scottish hillside, robbing James of his uncle, his cousin and his elder brother, and thus propelling his father into the ermine of the thirteenth Marquess. The family was still trying to come to terms with their loss, and the many adjustments that now had to be made.

James insisted on continuing to be known as Mr Montrayne, even though tradition now bestowed on him the courtesy title of Earl of Aullton. Abby, on the other hand, quite liked being Lady Abigail Montrayne, except when she remembered how she'd acquired the title, at which point she'd burst into tears.

Successfully containing his own grief, James was sensitive to his little girl's bouts of sadness and, for the moment at least, when she wanted something that would distract her, he let her have her way.

He had already bought a birthday card for Rachel Childers, wife of one of the tenant farmers on his Newton Hall estate, but little Abby had decided that she wanted to buy her own. It made sense. Debbie, Rachel's daughter, had been Abby Montrayne's best friend for as long as either of the girls could remember and, since James was a widower, Rachel had been something of a mother figure to the young child.

Newton Hall itself no longer existed, having succumbed to a disastrous fire in the nineteen thirties, but the estate still flourished in the hands of a competent business manager. James and his daughter lived in the Dower House about a mile from the site of the old hall, looked after by Doris Siddons, housekeeper to James just as she had been to his godmother before him. The location of the Dower House was idyllic, but scenic tranquillity did sometimes have its drawbacks. The nearest shop with anything like a decent selection of cards was over in Uttoxeter, which wasn't really a problem, except that James had completely forgotten that Wednesday was market day.

All of which meant that parking the car turned out to be something of a nightmare, and they ended up leaving the Maserati in a side street some distance from the town centre. On their walk to the card shop, Abby managed to cajole her father into believing that a slice of rich chocolate cake lathered with hot fudge sauce would make a good substitute for the lunch Mrs Siddons would offer them back at the Dower House.

It was while they were sitting in the coffee shop, Abby part way through her cake, and James munching on a sausage roll, that they heard the sound of sirens.

"Police?" queried Abby, another spoonful half way to her mouth. "Or maybe an ambulance."

"Or maybe a fire-engine," said James, his ears picking up the sound of a heavy diesel engine, revving hard.

"You win," conceded Abby, as a large, red shape sped past the window of the café.

She twisted her head around, trying to see where the fire appliance was going.

"What do you think's happened, Dad," she asked.

"Don't know, sweetheart," he replied. "Let's just hope it's not too bad."

It was a forlorn hope, as they discovered on their way back to the car.

Their route would have taken them across the Market Place, except that it was now blocked off by police cars, and no-one was being allowed through. James felt Abby pulling at his hand as she tried to see what was going on.

Standing six foot four inches, James could see over the heads of most people, and with a bulk of over two hundred and thirty pounds, he could elbow his way through the rest. Not that bulk was needed on this occasion. He could see all too clearly the cause of the disturbance.

One of the row of shops on the far side of the Market Place was fiercely ablaze. Its frontage was so scarred and blackened by the flames erupting from its windows that it was impossible to read its sign. It didn't matter. James knew the shop. Concerned about backing up the files on his laptop, he had bought an external hard drive from Byte Store Networks only a few months previously.

Newton-under-Grangewood – 2:55 pm

The bus set Richard down outside the village shop. If he'd missed it, there wouldn't have been another one until tomorrow. Since he was the only passenger to alight, the bus company probably had ample justification for reducing its service through the village.

Slinging his backpack over his shoulder, Richard moved quickly into the shelter of the shop's recessed doorway. It wasn't the weather he was sheltering from, but prying eyes which he feared might have reached the village ahead of him. He had noticed several cars parked by the green, and he now scrutinized them carefully to see whether any appeared to be occupied. As far as he could tell, they were all empty, so he turned his attention to the few pedestrians in sight.

The two middle-aged ladies chatting by the church gate seemed vaguely familiar, and his gaze passed quickly over them. A tall man in a dark suit who was walking towards them held his attention for a moment until he realised it was the vicar. A young woman leading a toddler by the hand was quickly discounted, as

14

was the elderly gentleman strolling past the green with an equally elderly cavalier spaniel in tow.

And that seemed to be the sum total of current village life. No lurking strangers, or anyone who Richard's over-active imagination could consider suspicious. No-one was taking the slightest interest in him, or so he thought.

"Richard? Is that you?"

The voice came from behind him, and his head snapped round, fear written large on his ashen features.

Irene Sparrow, owner of the shop, was peering at him anxiously through the half-opened door. He hadn't heard the latch click open, but maybe the door hadn't been properly closed anyway. He'd been so busy concentrating on the street that he hadn't noticed.

"Are you all right, dear," she asked, real concern in her voice.

"Er… … yes… …yes… … Can I come in?"

Richard pushed passed her without waiting for an answer.

"Yes, dear, of course," said Mrs Sparrow, stepping hastily aside. "The shop's open 'til seven, as you very well know."

She had helped to manage the village store ever since her husband had inherited the business from his parents. She and the store had survived both the death of her husband and the decision of the Post Office to close its branch in the village. At first, the reduction in her income had hit hard, but an understanding landlord had ensured that the village need not lose its shop along with its Post Office. The Newton Hall Estate kept her rent at a level that enabled her to run the shop efficiently and at a modest profit, to the benefit of both villagers and shopkeeper.

Mrs Sparrow had known Richard ever since he had come to live with his grandmother at Rainbow Cottage following the death of his parents. She remembered him as being always a little odd, so she took no offence at his abrupt manner.

"Is there something you're wanting, dear?" she asked, closing the door quietly.

Since, for the moment, there were no other potential customers in the shop, Richard had her full attention.

He looked around vaguely, not even sure why he had come into the shop in the first place. It must have been the shock of having Mrs Sparrow appear so suddenly behind him that had startled him into unconscious action.

"Er... ... don't know," he replied. "Just a minute."

"You take your time, dear. There's no hurry."

"OK," he said. Then he decided to add, very much as an afterthought, but just as his parents had taught him, "Thanks."

She nodded amiably and, having nothing better to do for the moment, watched him curiously. Being a lady for whom conversation, when possible, was far preferable to silence, she searched her mind for something to say.

As he stared at a large basket of bread, freshly delivered that morning, she found it.

"There was a man in here earlier. Asking for you, he was."

She might be used to Richard's odd behaviour, but she was nevertheless surprised by the speed with at which he spun round.

"It's all right, dear," she said calmingly, troubled by an expression she'd never seen on his face before. "He was only asking about computers... ... said he'd been told you were good with them."

Her words didn't seem to be having the soothing effect she had intended.

"Really, dear," she went on. "It was nothing. He said he'd got one needing repairing... ... thought you might help... ... I told him to look for you at the shop up in Uttoxeter."

Richard stared at her, his lips moving slightly but no words came out.

"That was all right, dear, wasn't it?" she asked, genuinely concerned now.

She reached out a hand to try and reassure him, but he flinched away. He'd never liked being touched, she remembered now.

"He was a stranger," she said, still trying to be helpful. "Talked with a funny accent... ... Polite enough, even though he didn't look very friendly... ...He said he thought he might find you at your grandma's. That's why he came in. To ask where Rainbow Cottage is. I told him you wouldn't be there... ...You visited on Sunday and your grandma told me you'd gone back to work. Anyway, you never come down here in the week... ... only at weekends."

She paused and her brow creased as she remembered what day it was.

"But... ... you're here today... ... Has something happened to your grandma?"

She watched in amazement as Richard stared wildly around him and then bolted for the back of the shop and the door that led through into the store-room.

She was still frozen in place when she heard the slamming of the back door to the premises as Richard made his escape into her garden.

"Well!" she exclaimed to her empty store. "Did you ever... ...?"

River Ash, Grangewood – 3:40 pm

The river was not wide. In fact, some folk would probably have thought it nothing more than a stream. On the other hand, it was at least ten feet across at its narrowest point, and was sufficiently fast flowing to avoid the formation of stagnant pools. Roughly paralleling the right bank, a couple of yards from the edge, ran a public footpath, clearly identified by way-markers at strategic points. Unobservant hikers following this path might have thought that they were walking through an area of well-established woodland bisected by the river. More observant eyes would have noticed that, while true, this was not the whole story.

The trees on the path's side of the river had grown up haphazardly, fairly close together, with plenty of ground litter and sprawling undergrowth. On the other bank, where no path was evident, the trees were widely spaced, with nothing more than mown grass showing between them. Beside the path, the hiker might identify many native species, oak and ash predominating,

17

but over the water giant redwoods rubbed shoulders with Monterey Pine and Douglas Fir. Between their trunks, far away from the bank, anyone nosey enough to be looking would make out the unmistakable shapes of majestic cedars of Lebanon.

Richard had no interest in the trees, nor the song of the birds flitting between them. He was equally oblivious to the rippling splashes coming from the river as water dashed against boulders rising above the surface. His attention was entirely focussed on trying to pick up any indications of pursuit over the thudding of his heart and the sound of panting as his lungs drew in deep breaths.

The back garden of the village store had a gate giving access to a narrow lane which Richard had used to make his way round to the rear of his grandma's cottage. Something told him that, if he could, he ought to make sure that she was all right. He was satisfied on that score when he caught sight of her taking in the dry washing that had been hanging out on the line. It had been so tempting to rush forward at that moment and take refuge in his old bedroom, but he knew that this was a temptation that needed resisting. They clearly knew where his grandma lived and, just as clearly, they would find him if he stayed.

He had crept away without allowing her to see him, having some vague notion that if she didn't see him then she wouldn't have to lie to protect him, and she would therefore be safe. It sounded logical enough. He just hoped it was true.

The trouble was… … he had nowhere else to go.

Rainbow Cottage backed onto the river, almost. Only the public footpath separated her garden fence from the river bank. As his grandma had entered the house with her basket full of washing, Richard had ducked down and kept below the level of the fence as he tried to creep past without being seen.

All would have been well if one of his pursuers had not decided to take a look at the rear of Rainbow Cottage. Even so, Richard almost made it. His pursuer's attention was so much focussed on the garden and windows of the cottage that he did not, at first, notice the figure several hundred yards along the footpath.

Richard, constantly looking back, saw him first.

And he ran.

Which was a mistake.

The sudden flash of movement caught the pursuer's attention, and Richard heard shouts behind him confirming that he'd been spotted.

He ran faster.

He kept to the path because the going was easier, and he knew that he had the advantage. At school, he had never been able to master the concept of working together at team sports but, left to himself, he could run faster than anyone else he knew.

And so he ran, for over three miles, dodging the occasional dog-walker or fisherman, until the heaving of his lungs and the pain in his side brought him to a reluctant stop.

Newton Hall Dower House – 4:05 pm

Abby Montrayne peered out from behind the magnificent trunk of a Wellingtonia. She watched the young man slow to a walk, stagger a few steps, and then bend forward to rest his hands on his knees.

She was all alone. She knew that she had wandered farther from the house than she was supposed to, but she was still within the grounds of the Dower House. She hadn't strayed out into the wider estate beyond the boundary formed, at this point, by the River Ash.

She didn't flinch when she heard the unmistakable sound of a gunshot. They were hardly a rarity in the countryside around here.

The young man, on the other hand, straightened immediately and looked back along the path in the direction from which he had come. Abby watched as he then looked around in all directions, his gaze eventually settling on a narrow bridge which crossed the river about twenty yards from where he stood. The bridge might be narrow and wooden, but it was sturdily made, as Abby well knew. She had often played Pooh-Sticks there with her dad, or Mrs Siddons, or Debbie or whoever else was willing to keep her company.

The young man ran to the bridge and tried to open the gate that barred access to it from his side of the river. Finding it securely locked, he then vaulted over it, ignoring the clearly painted sign that announced that the land on the other side of the bridge was private.

Abby was more curious than frightened, but she kept the tree between her and the strange young man as he ran up from the river bank in the direction of the Dower House. Why he should be doing this, she couldn't imagine. Then she noticed his frequent glances behind him as he ran, and it dawned on her young mind that someone was chasing him.

More interested than ever, she turned her attention back to the river. She watched for what seemed to her like ages, but she saw nothing out of the ordinary.

It was a shame that she turned away when she did, curious about where the young man thought he was going. Had she watched for only a few seconds longer, she would have seen a tall, heavily-built man stagger into view, pause, and finally lean against a tree as he fought to get his breath back.

Abby may not have seen *him*, but her red, fleecy jacket was not ideal camouflage amongst the greens and browns of the parkland. As she moved, the flash of colour caught the breathless man's eye and he watched, chest heaving, as the red shape disappeared among the trees on the far side of the river. He couldn't see clearly, but for some time now he'd been following a red backpack as it bounced on the shoulders of his quarry. He straightened up and reached for his phone.

Abby was on her way back to the house, eyes alert for any sign of the young man, when she heard her father calling.

"Abby... ... Abby.... ... Where are you? Come here now!"

There were times when she'd turn her father's search into a game, and she'd dance from tree to bush around him. However, his tone of voice made it clear that this was not to be one of those times.

"Abby."

She ran in the direction of his voice and saw him within seconds. She also saw the young man, struggling feebly to free himself from the grip of a worried and very angry James Montrayne.

Newton Hall Dower House – 8:35 pm

Of course, there had to be explanations.

When Richard was scared, or felt himself to be under unbearable pressure, he would do one of two things. He would either clam up completely, his most common response, shutting down all input from the outside world around him, or he would gabble incessantly, hurling out a barrage of words at the source of his distress.

His default response was already powering up, when some words in a child's voice had penetrated his terrified mind.

"Daddy… … what are you doing with that man?"

The sight of a little girl peering at him curiously had opened the floodgates in his mind to allow a torrent of words to come tumbling out.

It had taken much of the evening to make sense of it all but, by the time Abby had taken herself off to get ready for bed, James thought he had a fairly clear idea of what had happened. Sitting with Richard in the conservatory, his favourite room for relaxing quietly, James said, "Let me just check that I've got this straight."

Richard was sitting still, right on the edge of his chair, resisting the impulse to start rocking back and forth. Sensing that James's comment needed a response, he nodded slowly.

"OK, then," said James, reaching for his coffee mug from the low table in front of him. "You repaired a computer for some haulage company but, instead of leaving the dud part behind, you took it with you."

Richard nodded again, but didn't say anything. James sipped his coffee, and continued.

"It was a hard drive with lots of stuff stored on it... ... some company stuff... ...and some other stuff... ... You know that because you did what you shouldn't have done, and examined the hard drive back at the shop."

Richard shook his head.

"No... ... At home."

"OK," said James. "At home then... ... And although the hard drive was damaged, you were able to lift off a number of files... ... How exactly do you do that, by the way? No, don't tell me. We'll maybe come to that later."

There was almost a sparkle in Richard's eyes as he considered his achievement.

"It wasn't easy," he said eagerly.

"I'm sure it wasn't," agreed James, "especially as a number of those files were encrypted... ... That is what you said, isn't it?"

Richard nodded and the sparkle seemed to fade slightly.

"And you managed to... ... what's the word... ... decrypt them?"

"It took time," offered Richard. "But we were on holiday... ...so I had plenty. Anyway, I'm good at things like that. You probably wouldn't believe some of......"

He stopped, as though afraid of saying too much.

"I'm sure I believe that you're very capable," said James, taking another sip of his coffee. He gestured to Richard to do the same, but the boy ignored his mug which was gradually cooling on the table.

"At what point," pursued James, "did you realise that these encrypted files related to some sort of criminal activity?"

"Not at first," admitted Richard. "But then I started matching the encrypted files to the open files... ...Dates and amounts of money in the encrypted files related to Simpkins Logistics trucks returning from the Continent. There were lots of shipments recorded in the open files, so I wondered what was special about these other shipments that they needed to be kept hidden."

"And you decided on... ...?"

James already knew the answer, but waited for Richard to spell it out.

"It was obvious… … Had to be drugs or people or guns… … or maybe all of them."

"So which is it?" asked James.

"I don't know yet," said Richard, as though admitting to some sort of failure. "But I'll work it out, given enough time."

It was James's turn to nod.

"I rather believe you will," he said. "But time seems to be in short supply. From what you have told me, the owners of those files want them back… … probably because they don't want them to fall into the hands of the authorities. I can't believe they wouldn't have had backups."

Richard nodded slowly, but looked puzzled as he thought about the men who had been chasing him.

"How did they know about my grandma?" he asked. "How did they know where she lived?"

James was fairly sure that he knew the answer.

"Your boss at the computer shop."

"Tim wouldn't have told them," said Richard emphatically.

"He probably would… … if they were hurting him enough."

Richard clearly didn't understand, and James suddenly realised why the boy had never mentioned the fire at the computer shop.

"You don't know, do you?" he said.

"Know what?"

So James told him about the fire, and about his brief conversation with the senior fire officer on site. He told him about arson, and probable murder.

Richard was watching him in stunned amazement when the ringing of a telephone cut through the silence. It was the landline. James glanced at the extension but decided to ignore it.

The ringing stopped, but after a couple of minutes it started again. James was rising from his chair to answer it when, once again, it stopped. Richard seemed not to have noticed. His eyes were wide and his mouth was open, but no words came out. James was beginning to worry about him, when Bill Siddons, who had been butler to James's godmother, put his head round the door.

"What is it, Bill?" asked James, using the name by which his most senior retainer had been known for almost all his life. Siddons had been christened Walter, which at school had inevitably become shortened to Walt. It had been a short leap from that to Walt Disney, then famous for Mickey Mouse and thence, due to Walt's rather prominent upper teeth, to Goofy. Walt had been bearable, but Goofy most definitely was not. When he had been evacuated along with many other children during the Second World War, he had told everyone that his given name was Bill, and it had stuck.

"Sorry to disturb you, sir. But Professor Walcott phoned to confirm that she'll be travelling down on Friday to accompany you to the Lord Lieutenant's Gala Ball on Saturday evening. I will, of course, see that her usual room is made ready."

"Thank you, Bill... ... Was there anything else?"

"Indeed, sir. A gentleman is asking to speak to you. Most insistent he is. He says it's about some property that you need to restore to him."

Thursday

24th April 2003

Newton Hall Dower House – 9:40 am

After James had been up to Abby's room for her usual bedtime routine of chat, story and prayers, he and some good friends of his had sat up late into the night talking over with Richard the implications of the earlier phone call.

The caller had given no name and his conversation had been firm but polite. He knew, he said, that James had a guest staying with him who had arrived sometime that afternoon, bringing a particular item of property with him. The caller said that he would be pleased to meet this guest so that he could restore that property to its rightful owner. The caller said that he had no wish to trouble Lord Aullton or his family, so if Richard could make his way to his grandmother's house by eight thirty in the morning, then that would be an end of the matter.

Recognising the clear threat to Richard's grandma, James had immediately contacted his friend Andy Graham, CEO of Rapid Response International Security Consultants. Andy might manage the company, but it had been James's money that had helped set it up and, as Chairman of the company, he knew he could always call for support whenever he needed it. Its employees had all served in some branch of the armed forces, a few even serving with James himself in the Royal Marines. They were more than competent. Tough and resourceful, they were the ideal people to have on hand in a difficult situation.

Two of them had been watching grandma's house throughout the night, having first ascertained that she was safe and well. She believed, on answering her door to a late caller, that she had been turning away a political campaigner conducting a survey. Since Grandma didn't exactly appreciate a knock on her door so late in the evening, the sitting MP was almost sure to be one vote down come the next election.

Andy, and two others, had spent the night at the Dower House, at first talking, and then watching and patrolling, just in case. He and Richard were now sitting with James in the library. James was supposed to be driving Abby over to Heighley Grange Farm to spend the day with her friend Debbie, and the ponies they kept stabled there, but he had now delegated that chauffeuring duty to Bill Siddons.

A sleepless night had done Richard absolutely no good at all. If anything, he was even more terrified now that it had fully sunk in just how ruthless his pursuers were. He had never been great on self-awareness, but there was a suspicion lurking in his mind, which he couldn't shake off, that he had brought this mess down on himself.

"So what's next, James?" asked Andy.

He brushed a crumb from the front of his shirt and took another bite of his bacon sandwich, thoughtfully brought to the library by Mrs Siddons. He had missed breakfast since he'd been down in the village visiting Grandma.

For the occasion, from a selection of fake IDs, he had chosen that of an official of the local council, explaining to Grandma that he was calling early since he was on his way into work. She had accepted this without question, particularly when he explained that there was good reason to believe that she had been overpaying her council tax and was due for a rebate. He had been in the house from ten minutes to eight until nine fifteen, helped along by the fact that Grandma was a great talker.

At eight sixteen, he had received a call on his cell phone saying that an old model Honda Accord had driven into the village and parked along the road from Grandma's cottage. At eight thirty-five, there had been a knock on Grandma's door. Someone with a foreign accent had asked if Richard was home. Grandma had told him that Richard was in Uttoxeter. She hadn't seen him since the weekend. The stranger had said that he was expecting to meet Richard in the village that morning, and asked if it would be OK to come in and wait. Grandma had told him she was busy with a man from the council, and anyway Richard had a job in Uttoxeter, and he wouldn't be coming to the village again until Sunday when she expected him for lunch.

The mention of the man from the council seemed to work the magic that Andy had hoped and the stranger had retreated to his Accord. He had sat in the car for half an hour, watching

Grandma's house, eventually driving off at five minutes past nine.

"Did you get a good look at the guy at the door?" asked James.

"Sure, and he saw me. I guess he was looking for any sign of you... ..."

He waved his bacon sandwich in Richard's direction.

"Anyway, I'd got some papers spread over the table, and I think it all looked pretty kosher."

He took a small bite while he thought, and then added, "I reckon he'd have forced his way in if I'd not been there."

There was a small sound from Richard which he ignored.

"Nat was doing the fisherman thing round the back of Grandma's... ...not too close... ...some way along the bank. There was a second guy in the car and he went round the back of Grandma's and watched for half-an-hour or so. Nat kept an eye on him while John watched the front. The jammy sod actually caught a fish while this guy was standing there."

"Any good?" asked James.

"I'd say," replied Andy. "Rainbow trout it was. That's why Grandma's cottage is called Rainbow Cottage... ... Nothing to do with the sky apparently. Trout seem to like lurking along that stretch of water... ... One of the many things I learnt from her while I was there... ... which reminds me... ... Sitting talking to her for a while, it was obvious she's not well off. Now we've raised her hopes about a refund on her council tax, you'd better make sure a dollop of cash finds its way to her door."

"Good point," James acknowledged. "I'll see it's done."

Andy nodded and turned his attention back to his sandwich. He chewed thoughtfully, his eyes on Richard who sat slumped in his chair by the window. The boy seemed to Andy to be motionless, detached and uninvolved in what was happening in the room, until he looked into the young man's eyes. They were constantly on the move, roving ceaselessly around the room without ever focussing on another person. Andy wondered what was going on behind those eyes. Was the boy's mind a blank, or was his head full of complex thoughts, tumbling feverishly around as they tried to find a way to be expressed?

Mystified, Andy shook his head before turning to James to say, "I know I asked this last night, but I didn't really get an answer. Just what has this kid got himself into... ... and why are we bothered?"

James thought about that, just as he had done the previous evening.

"I could probably answer part of that," he said, "but let's check with the office and see what they've found out first."

RRISC Central Office, Birmingham – 9:55 am

Rod Taylor had been up all night, and wasn't entirely sure just what he'd got to show for it. Not that he minded being called into the office for an all-nighter. He'd probably have been awake anyway, most of the time. The nightmares saw to that. A hostage extraction had gone wrong a few months back, when an RPG had exploded under his armoured Jeep. The hostage had survived but one of his team had been badly burned getting her out of the vehicle. If Rod had got his arse in gear, they might all have got safely away, but he'd frozen up while his team mate played the hero. He couldn't explain it then, and he still couldn't, but it was eating him up that he'd let his mate down, and the guy was still in hospital months after the event.

So Rod didn't venture into the field anymore. He stayed at the office immersing himself in his new role as head of RRISC's IT division. It suited him perfectly, and he excelled at it, but it couldn't deal with his nightmares. Except for last night, when lack of sleep had ensured their absence.

The phone on his desk started ringing so he swivelled his chair slightly to reach for the handset, glancing at the phone's display panel as he did so.

"Morning, Boss," he said, greeting James in his usual manner.

"Morning, Rod. The phone's on speaker. Andy's with me. What have you got for us?"

30

There were three computer monitors on his desk and, as Rod tapped a few keys, the screen on the right hand monitor changed. He read off from the display.

"First off, Simpkins Logistics is a kosher firm. Simpkins Logistics and Freight Forwarding International, to give it its full name. SLAFFI for short. First registered as a limited company five years ago and, according to Companies House, their accounts are up to date. One director, one shareholder, name of... ... Bohdan Simonenko. Goes by the name of Danny Simpkins but, as far as I can tell, there's been no legal name change."

"Has he got any form?" asked Andy.

"I tried our police liaison this morning, soon as I thought he'd be awake. He came up zilch. Nothing known against this guy under either name."

"Squeaky clean, then," put in James.

"Not exactly," said Rod, lighting up his left hand monitor. "I've spent the night trawling across Europe......"

"Flying like Superman."

Andy's voice came across faintly in what was obviously an aside to James.

"Even faster," Rod quipped back, "especially with these babies... ... Anyway, with a name like Bohdan Simonenko, I thought I'd start in the old Eastern Bloc. Took a while, but there's a Bohdan Simonenko made a bit of a name for himself in Ukraine. Nothing proved... ... no convictions... ... but a whole shitload of rumours. Bottom line... ... anything that'll make him money, he'll do it... ... and he doesn't care who gets hurt."

"Sounds like he could be our guy," said James. "Good work, Rod."

"Thanks, Boss," replied Rod. "But I've got a bit more. I ran a check on director names and good old Bohdan comes up as owning two other haulage firms, one in Norfolk and another up near Liverpool. All set up about the same time, and all up to date with their accounts."

"Hmmm."

The grunt from Richard caused James to cast a look in his direction.

31

"Did you want to say something?" he asked.

Richard shook his head and looked down at the carpet.

"Have you had a look at these accounts?" asked James, turning his attention back to Rod.

"Sure. I paid up and downloaded copies from Companies House. I've emailed them to you."

Rod paused, tapped at his keyboard and a set of accounts appeared on the centre monitor.

"I'm no expert, Boss, but these accounts look solid to me. I'm guessing here... ...but what I'm thinking is... ...if this guy's dirty, he keeps one set of accounts, all legit, to keep HMRC happy... ..."

Andy finished the thought for him.

"... ...and another set to keep track of the dirty money."

Newton Hall Dower House – 10:35 am

James fired up his laptop while Rod was still on the phone and together they examined the three sets of accounts which had been emailed across. Andy peered over his shoulder and they discussed them for a while with Rod tossing in extra titbits of information which he had uncovered about Simonenko's companies.

It was a discussion to which Richard contributed nothing until James printed off copies for him to look at. Up to that point, he had just sat hunched in his chair, watching and listening, but keeping his mouth firmly closed.

Two minutes after he had taken the papers in his hands, he spoke in a voice so quiet that the others hardly heard him.

"These are the open files."

Andy glanced at him.

"What was that?"

"These figures," said Richard, a little louder. "They're from the open files."

"You sure?" asked James.

Richard nodded, but Andy looked sceptical. Richard's backpack was at his feet, but he'd taken nothing out of it. All he had in his hands were the papers James had given him.

"How do you know?" Andy asked him.

Richard raised his right hand and tapped his temple with his middle finger.

"I just do," he said. "It's all in here."

James frowned. "And the encrypted files?"

"They're in here too."

Richard was not good at reading other people's emotions, but even he could tell that neither of his listeners was convinced.

"Would you like to see?" he asked.

Rod's voice came from the speaker.

"What's going on there?"

"Tell you what, Rod," said James. "We'll give you a call back shortly."

He ended the call, and said to Richard, "Show us."

The boy reached for his backpack saying, "I'll need to borrow your laptop."

He extracted a slim, rectangular box with a cable attached.

"The hard drive's in here… … Can I… …?"

He reached for the laptop, so James placed it on an ancient-looking desk saying, "Gather round."

He let Richard have the chair and he and Andy stood to either side.

"I just need to… …"

Richard plugged the cable from the hard drive into one of the laptop's USB ports.

"And then… …"

He located a second port and plugged in a USB memory stick.

"The program I wrote to decrypt the files is on there," he explained.

"Now, all we need to do is… …"

They all waited. Andy and James seemed completely mystified, but Richard, now in his element, exuded confidence.

But before he could show them anything, the phone rang.

Dakers Lodge, Staffordshire – 10:50 am

Bohdan Simonenko, AKA Danny Simpkins, loved Victorian Gothic, which is why he'd made his home in the secluded country house of a former Victorian carpet manufacturer.

William Henry Dakers had accumulated a substantial fortune; his son had just about maintained it; his grandson had spent it; his great-grandson had gone bankrupt and Dakers Lodge had been put up for auction. The house, in an isolated location on the edge of the Staffordshire moorlands, set in five acres of gardens, was exactly what Simonenko had been looking for.

In the past five years, he had made it entirely his own, complete with top-level security and the best communication system civilian money could buy.

That communication system was about to earn its keep.

"Mr Montrayne," said Simonenko, "or should I address you as Lord Aullton."

Simonenko was immensely proud of his English. He had worked so hard on intonation, pronunciation and idiom that there was barely a trace of Eastern European in his accent.

"Montrayne will do," he heard in reply. "So what should I call you?"

"If you must have a name, you may call me William," Simonenko told him, thinking of the Lodge's first owner.

"OK, William, what do you want?"

"You know very well what I want, Mr Montrayne. My associates had a wasted journey this morning, so I assume you are still entertaining your guest."

"I am indeed... ... William... ... and I should tell you that his stay is likely to be... ... prolonged. Especially as his workplace has gone up in flames."

Simonenko breathed hard. He was trying to keep his temper in check since losing it would clearly serve no useful purpose.

"Ah, yes. I heard about that. Very sad… … and yet, it shows, does it not, just how easily tragedy can strike any one of us?"

There was silence for a moment before Montrayne's voice could be heard again.

"All the more reason for my guest to stay here where he knows he is safe."

"I am sorry to hear you say that, Mr Montrayne. You see, I really am anxious to make his acquaintance and to… … retrieve the property he has been taking care of for me… … No, no, Mr Montrayne. Please listen. Do not interrupt… …You may be tempted to involve other… … authorities, but I would strongly advise against it."

"And what if I have already done so?" Montrayne managed to break in.

"I know you have not," replied Simonenko with certainty, thinking of an aging police sergeant and an inspector on the verge of retirement, both of whose bank accounts were far healthier than they had any right to be.

The silence that greeted these words was taken by the Ukrainian to be a good sign.

"I am going to suggest an alternative rendezvous, Mr Montrayne and I would further suggest that it would be in your own best interests to ensure that this time your guest does not fail to keep the appointment."

He lowered the tone of his voice before adding, "I hope this is all perfectly clear to you… … You will escort your guest to… …"

"That's not going to happen…… William," Montrayne interrupted. "My guest is enjoying his stay here, and I would suggest that you get used to the idea."

Simonenko was about to tell James Montrayne that he was making a big mistake, when he realised that the connection had been broken.

He swore, softly because he had guests in residence who had no idea their host was anything other than a moderately successful, but generally mild-mannered businessman. It was a carefully crafted illusion which he made every effort not to dispel.

Newton Hall Dower House – 11:15 am

The first item for discussion as soon as James put the phone down was the identity of the caller. Could it have been Simonenko himself? Since Richard had never met the boss of Simpkins Logistics, he was little help, except for confirming that everyone he had met who was connected with the firm had a definite East European accent.

Rod was given the job of trying to establish where the call had come from. No-one had any real hope that he'd succeed, but it had to be tried.

While Richard focussed all his attention on the laptop, Andy said to James, "Did you notice how he spoke... ... how carefully he phrased everything?"

James nodded.

"He made sure we understood exactly what he meant, without actually saying anything that could really incriminate him."

"Do you suppose he thought we were recording him?" asked Andy.

"We probably should have been," said James, wishing he'd thought of it and prepared for it.

"Next time," said Andy. "I'll get onto it."

He pulled out his cell phone and called the RRISC office. While he was sorting out the wire-tap, James used the house phone to call Mrs Siddons and arrange for coffee ASAP and lunch about twelve-thirty.

The next thing they needed to consider was whether to involve the police and, if so, what to tell them. Richard was clearly scared by the very mention of the police and, although James and Andy both tried to convince him that he'd done nothing wrong, he didn't seem convinced.

"Trouble is," said Andy, once Mrs Siddons had delivered the coffee, and Richard had settled again to the laptop, "this guy sounds as if he has someone in the police on his payroll. Maybe more than one. He was too confident that he'd know if we contacted them."

He and James had barely begun to consider the implications of that when Richard called their attention to the laptop screen. First he displayed two windows side by side, one showing the accounts submitted to Companies House, and the other showing the accounts displayed in what he called the open files.

He was right. They matched completely.

Then he brought up another screen.

"What's this?" asked James.

"It's a combined roster of the three haulage companies. You can see them referenced in this column here and… …"

"Hang on a minute," James interrupted. "Where did you get that? Is this another of those open files?"

For a moment, Richard didn't move, and then he shook his head slowly.

"So it's one of the encrypted files?"

Richard shook his head again.

"All right then," said James, exasperated. "Where did it come from?"

There was silence again before Richard spoke, without taking his eyes from the screen.

"It's on my memory stick. I hacked their computers."

James and Andy stared at him in amazement. In the end, it was James who was first to speak.

"You hacked them," he said. "So you knew about these other two companies before Rod told us."

"Er… …yeah… …I guess."

"You guess," said Andy. "Don't you realise hacking can get you into a whole load of trouble."

"Not if you know what you're doing."

"Well I guess," said Andy, "that Gary McKinnon thought he knew what he was doing when he hacked the US military last year, and now look at the trouble he's in."

"The name's familiar but I can't quite place it," said James.

"It was the back end of last year," Andy told him. "Grand Jury indictment with seven counts of computer hacking. The US doesn't take kindly to having its military computer systems shut down."

"Can't really blame them for that," replied James.

"No," agreed Andy. "And you've got to be really good to get in and out of other people's systems without leaving your fingerprints all over the place... ... digitally speaking, that is."

James gave him a look, and then reached out to draw him close before whispering, "Are we that good?"

"I'm not," replied Andy, in an equally quiet voice. "But Rod is, and that new kid he's training could well be even better. RRISC's policy is only to use hacking as a last resort, and then only if we're certain nothing can be traced back to us."

"You guys finished?" Richard interrupted. "Coz there's stuff here you need to see."

"OK, show us," said James.

So he did, and the ensuing discussion extended well into the afternoon.

Newton Lane, Staffordshire – 3:45 pm

Abby was slumped down in the back seat of the Vauxhall Omega Elite as it turned out of the drive to Heighley Grange Farm. She'd had a great day with her friend Debbie. They had played together, collected eggs, fed lambs and groomed their ponies. After lunch, as soon as Debbie's mum was free to supervise them, they had practised their riding together. But all good things must come to an end, and now it was time to return to the Dower House.

Bill Siddons was driving, which was quite usual for him these days. His job had latterly become much more that of chauffeur than butler, contrary to his entry on the estate's payroll. James Montrayne didn't seem to want all the pomp and ceremony which had so delighted his godmother, Lady Helena Marchmont.

She, however, had been born before the First World War, when the domestic arrangements of country houses were far more strictly regimented than she had observed in her later years. She had not approved of the change.

Nor had her butler, during her lifetime, but since James had come to the Dower House after Lady Helena's death some five years previously, Bill's formerly strict views had mellowed. His aching joints reminded him that he was getting older every day, and a certain easing of his workload had not come as too unpleasant a change.

Carefully manoeuvring the big car along the lane away from the farm, he told himself that he couldn't really complain at being asked to drive through some beautiful English countryside and actually be paid for doing it. A quick glance in his rear-view mirror showed that Abby had already fallen asleep.

He drove steadily, as he always did with such a precious bundle in the back, even though he was now well used to the car. James had bought it just over a year ago finding it rather more comfortable to drive than his godmother's Maserati, which hadn't been built with a man of his size in mind. Bill liked the car, though he had to remember to keep a light foot on the accelerator if he didn't want the Omega's 3.2 litre engine to power him through a hedge into a field.

The hedges remained intact for several miles, throughout which Abby remained fast asleep.

But that was due to change.

Her energy temporarily exhausted, Abby would have slept until they arrived back at the Dower House, but she was suddenly jolted awake when Bill Siddons slammed his foot hard on the Omega's brakes.

"What is it, Mr Bill?" she asked, more curious than frightened.

She had recently taken to calling him Mr Bill. In her young mind it had seemed disrespectful simply to call him Siddons, and she certainly couldn't call him by his first name, so Mr Bill it had become. She liked it and, apparently, so did he.

"What is it?" she asked again, leaning sideways to try and peer forward through the windscreen.

"Just hold tight, little miss," said Bill as he rammed the gear selector into reverse and stepped on the gas.

As the engine whine became a howl, Abby lifted her chin, trying to see what lay ahead. Men with masks over their faces were running towards them from a big, dark-coloured car which lay at an angle across the lane. They were yelling words that she didn't understand.

"Mr Bill, I'm scared."

"I know, honey," was all Bill could reply as he concentrated on what he planned to do next.

He swung the car's rear end into a field gateway, so fast that it demolished the well-rotted, wooden gate. Brakes again, then his fingers were fumbling with the gear selector. First gear, accelerator, spin the wheel and away.

Except they never made it.

As the Omega began to move forward, Abby heard several loud bangs like firecrackers on bonfire night. She screamed, and the car lurched as bullets shredded its nearside tyres.

Then the masked men were alongside the stationary car shouting at Bill to open the doors.

He refused, so they used the butts of their weapons to smash in the windows and release the door locks.

Hearing Abby screaming from behind him, Bill started to lash out as best he could from his cramped position behind the steering wheel, but not for long. The business end of a Walther P99 pressing into his cheek soon steadied him down.

Abby's cries were muffled now by the large hand clamped over her mouth. Other hands helped to drag her out of the back of the Omega and all Bill could do was watch as she was bundled into the rear of the black Range Rover which had so effectively blocked the road.

Bill watched, furious at his own impotence, as the Range Rover reversed to face down the lane away from him. The pistol jabbed harder into his cheek.

"You move and you die. Understand?"

Bill just stared ahead at the now stationary SUV, though his brain vaguely registered the trace of an accent in the voice. The pistol jabbed again.

"Understand?"

Bill licked his lips.

"I understand."

"Good. Now you tell Mr Montrayne, no police. We want simple exchange. He want his girl back, no police."

There was added vehemence in those last two words.

The pressure of the pistol eased.

"Mr Montrayne will hear from us. Remember… … do not move."

The man eased away and walked backwards to the Range Rover, all the time keeping his pistol pointed at Bill's head. As he neared it, the front passenger door opened and moments later the SUV was out of sight.

Bill reached into his jacket pocket for his mobile phone. He didn't like it, and hardly ever used it, but today he was glad of it. He just hoped that the battery had some life in it. His fingers trembled as he tried to press the right keys.

A phone some miles away began to ring.

From beginning to end, the whole business had lasted less than two minutes.

Dakers Lodge, Staffordshire – 4:10 pm

Bohdan Simonenko was seething.

His new strategy for the protection of his business interests, and for dealing with an interfering computer nerd, did not include the kidnapping of Lady Abigail Helena Montrayne, six-year-old daughter of the Earl of Aullton.

Simonenko had not remonstrated with Mykyta Shwetz over the burning of that shop in the centre of Uttoxeter. There had been a certain logic to that. The damage done to the owner needed to be covered up somehow, and if the missing hard drive was by some remote chance still on the premises, the fire would take care of it. But this time Shwetz had really surpassed himself for stupidity. It was characteristic of Simonenko that, at no point, did he blame himself for pushing Shwetz too hard, or for instilling so much fear in his subordinate that desperation overcame rational thinking. Shwetz was an idiot, pure and simple, and unreliable to the point of being downright dangerous. This latest demonstration of imbecility had escalated a minor problem right into the stratosphere.

Simonenko knew that he had to act swiftly and decisively if he was to haul this problem back to within manageable limits.

He reached for his phone, the special one with the voice changing facility and the capacity for relaying his call through so many ISPs that no-one had a chance of tracing it.

Newton Hall Dower House – 4:15 pm

James Montrayne was scared.

He had seen service in Northern Iraq in 1991, and later in Bosnia in 1995. He had seen human brutality at is worst, but nothing he had experienced had prepared him for what he was facing now. The death of his wife had been agonising, but at no time had the outcome of her condition depended on any decision he might make.

This was different. Any ill-considered response on his part now could mean the loss of his daughter.

He stared at the carpet of the conservatory, remembering Abby as she had been that morning, all togged up in her riding clothes for a day at the farm. And he asked himself, why her? What has she done to deserve this? He thought of all he did for his church, and he thought of Abby turning up every week for Sunday School. He remembered how much she enjoyed those lessons with Natalie Simmons, her teacher, and how she would share what she had learnt about God over Sunday lunch. And he asked himself, what is God thinking?

He became aware of Andy standing close beside his chair, and he felt a hand rest on his shoulder.

From somewhere through a fog, he heard Andy saying, "You can't blame yourself, James... ... You couldn't have known... ... I mean, there was just no way we could have known he'd go this far."

James nodded slowly. The fear was still there and wouldn't go away until Abby was safely back home again, but at least he was starting to think again. How long had the shock clouded his brain? He had no idea. He glanced up at the clock on the wall. The hands had barely moved since he had taken the call from Bill Siddons.

That was good. He told himself to keep calm, keep thinking. He told himself there was no reason for them to hurt his little girl, as long as they got what they wanted. He told himself he was going to get her back.

"Are John and Nat still around?" he asked.

"John's here. Nat's still watching Grandma," Andy told him.

"OK. Send John to pick up Bill, and organise a tow truck for the car."

"On it," said Andy, already pushing buttons on his cell phone.

"No police," murmured James to himself. "They told him no police."

He was still considering what to do about that when the house phone rang.

"Mr Montrayne," the voice said. "I am truly sorry for what you must be feeling at this moment."

You bastard, thought James, then reminded himself to keep calm, for Abby's sake.

"What do you want?" he asked bluntly.

"To restore your daughter to you, Mr Montrayne. You must be worried sick, so I think we should do this as soon as possible. An associate of mine, on some errand of his own, came across your little girl earlier this afternoon. He acted foolishly, as I'm sure you must agree, and instead of taking her home he called me to ask what he should do. Naturally, I told him he must restore her to you immediately, and that is what I have called to arrange."

"So what are you suggesting?" asked James, slightly reassured by the calm, business-like tone of the caller.

"I think that Blithfield reservoir would be convenient for both you and for my associate," said the voice. "There is a parking area at the east end of the causeway. If you can be there in… … say… … two hours' time, then this ordeal can be put behind you."

James was expecting more. There had to be a demand of some sort.

"Is that it?" he asked.

"Ah, Mr Montrayne, thank you so much. I was forgetting. Your young computer friend will be very keen to restore the property he has been taking care of for me. Perhaps you can bring him with you and we can, as it were, kill two birds with one stone. If you understand me."

There it was. Obliquely stated, but clear enough. Richard and the hard drive in exchange for Abby.

"I understand you perfectly," James told him. "We will see your associate at Blithfield at six-thirty."

"Excellent, Mr Montrayne. I am so glad to have been of assistance… … Oh, and by the way. For the sake of your daughter's good health, it would be best if we do this quietly. Any fuss would be very upsetting for her, as I'm sure you understand."

No police, you mean, thought James.

"I understand," he said. "No… … fuss."

Blithfield Reservoir – 6:25 pm

They were all set, but only just. The caller had allowed them enough time to do what he wanted, but not enough to get organised. At least, that's presumably what he hoped. Unfortunately for him, he hadn't allowed for the fact that James Montrayne had at his disposal the best kidnap and ransom team money could buy. Even so, it had been a rush job, and Andy

44

Graham hated rush jobs. Hasty planning made it all too easy to overlook some vital detail which had the potential to turn a great looking strategy into a total pig's breakfast.

The B5013 from Uttoxeter approached the reservoir almost at right angles, crossed via the half mile long causeway, and then continued on to Rugeley. It was not the busiest of country roads, bounded mostly by hedges and too narrow to merit a white line down its centre. The parking area lay beside an even narrower lane which turned left off the B-road just short of the causeway.

On the opposite side of the B-road from the turn-off lay a large field, and about one hundred yards into the field, majestic and solitary, stood a sturdy oak tree, full in its prime. Ten feet up in the tree, straddling a bough thicker than his waist, sat Peter Grant, a former sergeant in the SAS. He had a clear line of sight to the mouth of the turn-off. At that distance, this was point-blank range for the Barrett 82A1 .50 calibre rifle which rested comfortably along the branch supported by its bipod legs. To his left, and two feet higher up, crouched Pete's friend and colleague, Tim Rhodes. Tim was snuggled close in to the tree's massive trunk nursing an AWM from Accuracy International. The British-made Arctic Warfare Magnum rifle might not have the range of the Barrett, but in Tim's opinion this was more than compensated for by its light weight.

This was a volunteers-only job, and both men had signed up, but neither was happy.

Pete headed up RRISC's firearms training division which had contracts with various police authorities as well as the military. He was proud of the reputation they'd built up in just a few years, but all that was now in jeopardy should their activities this evening ever come to light. They were not just operating outside the terms of their licence. What they were preparing for now was downright illegal.

"This had better work," said Pete, almost to himself, as he peered down the telescopic sight atop the Barrett's barrel.

"If it doesn't, there's more than our jobs at stake," replied Tim. "I can't imagine what little Abby's feeling right now."

"She's the only reason I'm doing it," Pete told him, for the second or third time in the past hour.

They could not be sure what kind of vehicle the kidnappers would be using, but everyone was assuming that it would be the same SUV that took Abby in the first place. Pete and Tim's job was to stop it leaving if, for some reason, it was trying to take off with Abby or the computer kid on board.

Which would not be easy.

They would have to hit the engine and front tyres sideways-on, whichever way the vehicle turned as it came out of the parking area onto the road. They couldn't shoot before that, while the vehicle was head-on to them, not if there was the possibility that Abby or the kid might be inside.

Depending on circumstances, they might not be able to take the shot anyway, in which case there was backup in both directions. West, across the causeway, just outside the village of Admaston, a black Hummer H1 lay waiting, silent, sinister and massive. It might not be the most beautiful car in the world, but its three ton mass could certainly block the causeway if need be. To the east, up the road towards Abbots Bromley, a Ford Expedition was tucked against the hedge at the mouth of a narrow lane.

"We're as ready as we can be," said Pete, his eye still glued to the scope.

Not that he really needed it to see James pacing back and forth beside the Maserati, which had been reverse-parked so the car's elegant tail was towards the reservoir. However, the scope's lens also allowed him to see into the car where a young man, fidgety and scared, twisted and turned on the rear seat, looking first out of one window, then another.

"Do you think the Boss really means to hand that kid over in exchange for Abby?" asked Pete, twisting to glance up at Tim.

"Doubt it… … Not unless he has to, that is… … and that's where we come in. Their car's not leaving with Abby or the kid on board. If we can't take the shot, the guys down the road will do their stuff."

"Sounds like a plan," said Pete.

46

"Yeah… … and we all know what happens to plans."

"TUFF," said Pete, turning back to the scope.

That Unanticipated F*****g Factor had become something of a catchphrase around RRISC, which would probably have gladdened the heart of Helmuth von Moltke whose thesis on war is often simplistically misquoted as "No battle plan survives contact with the enemy".

"We're on," said Tim, from his slightly higher elevation. "Incoming ten-o'clock."

"Got it," replied Pete, and the two of them settled down to watch, to wait, and to ready themselves for the shot that both of them hoped they wouldn't have to take.

It was a black Range Rover, exactly as they'd been expecting.

It was approaching slowly, from the Abbots Bromley direction. They watched as the brake lights came on, and the big car turned into the lane. It swung around in a U-turn onto the parking area, and Pete found himself staring down his sights at the driver. He shifted his angle very slightly, but it was hard to see further into the vehicle because of the heavily tinted windows.

"Can you see Abby?" he asked, and there was a pause before Tim replied.

"Not from here… … It's those damn windows… … and she may be down on the floor."

Then both front doors opened and two men emerged. James was standing still, close to the front of the Maserati, and Pete wondered how much restraint he must be exercising not to leap forward and tear these guys in half.

Through his earpiece, he heard James ask, "Do you have my daughter?"

The passenger from the Range Rover seemed to be answering, but Pete couldn't hear his words.

Then James spoke again but Pete didn't catch what was said because the words were drowned by an urgent warning from Tim.

"Incoming… … two-o'clock."

A white Vauxhall Astra was approaching along the causeway. They expected it to carry on up the road towards Abbots Bromley or Uttoxeter but, as it neared the end of the causeway, it slowed and its right-hand turn light started blinking.

"Oh, shit!" muttered Pete as he caught sight of the driver just before the car made the turn into the lane.

"Trouble?" asked Tim.

"He's a cop."

"Bollocks… … TUFF again."

They could do nothing more than watch as the Astra swung smartly right into the first available spot in the parking area. It was nose-in to the grass, looking out over the water.

For several moments, nothing happened. James moved slowly to his left so that he could see the car and its occupant more clearly.

Pete heard him say, "That's nothing to do with us."

The guys from the Range Rover began backing up, hands reaching to open the doors.

"Wait," said James. "We can still do this."

Then the door of the Astra opened, and Pete saw the police officer climb out. He stood, leaving the door open, and looked out across the reservoir. Then he glanced over the roof of his car towards the Range Rover and the Maserati beyond it.

Something was grabbing the cop's attention, or maybe he was just naturally suspicious. Whatever it was, he started to walk around the back of the Astra towards the Range Rover.

Pete heard James call out to the cop, telling him to stay back, but the officer took no notice. James's warning probably only served to make him even more curious.

Nobody was ever going to find out what was going on in the policeman's mind. He made gestures which seemed to be telling everyone to stay exactly where they were, and then he reached up to his shoulder and his head tilted, ready to speak into his radio.

That did it.

The two guys scrambled into the Range Rover, while Pete and Tim could do no more than hold their breath.

They'd seen it in movies a thousand times and always wondered how anyone could be so stupid.

The police officer stood his ground in front of the Range Rover and raised both his hands in the air commanding it not to move.

It ignored him.

Watching through his scope, Pete saw the SUV lunge forward, and the cop hesitated for a second before trying to leap out of the way. It was only a second, but it made all the difference. The grill of the Range Rover struck him but, because of the way he was already twisting, he stumbled backwards rather than to the side. The SUV forged on, and Pete saw it lurch twice as first the front wheels, then the rear, ground over the cop's body.

"Shit… … Shit… … Shit!"

The surge of adrenaline and heightened heart beat were exactly the opposite of what a sniper tried for before taking a shot, but Pete steadied himself ready to do his best.

Then he heard James yelling, "Leave it, Pete… … Tim, leave it… … Stand down now."

Pete relaxed as he saw James run to the policeman, ominously still on the gravel of the parking area. In his earpiece, he heard James telling Cherry and Andy in the Ford Expedition that the Range Rover was coming their way. He didn't hear their reply as his ear-piece became dislodged while he was climbing down from his perch. Ramming it back in, he began methodically to pack away his gear.

"What a balls up," he said to Tim, as his colleague dropped to the ground beside him. "We'd better clear the area smartish. We don't want to get caught with these when the rest of the fuzz turns up."

"But what about Abby?" asked Tim.

"Andy'll get her," Pete told him confidently.

But Andy didn't.

Dakers Lodge, Staffordshire – 8.25 pm

Why was he surrounded by such incompetents?

It didn't occur to Bohdan Simonenko that, since he had chosen them himself, he ought to bear some responsibility for the proficiency level of his employees.

Their only redeeming feature perhaps was that they hadn't been caught. Some type of Ford SUV had tried to block their escape but, in his haste, the driver had misjudged it. Shwetz, on the other hand, hadn't. Seeing that the Ford was at something of an angle across the road, with a small gap between its rear and the hedge, Shwetz had put his foot down hard and aimed for the gap. Both the Ford and the Range Rover had suffered in the resulting collision, and the hedge had acquired a new opening, but the result had been satisfactory. The side wall of the Ford's front offside tyre had hit something sharp embedded in the verge and immediately ruptured, making pursuit impossible.

Even if the men in the Ford had succeeded in stopping Shwetz, it would not have helped them to recover the girl. She hadn't been in the Range Rover. Drugged and bound, she had been left in the boot of a stolen Honda Accord in a layby occasionally used by walkers needing somewhere to park their cars. Shwetz hadn't done everything wrong. He'd even changed the number plates on the Honda. If the exchange had gone according to plan, Shwetz would have told Montrayne where he could find his daughter.

The Range Rover's rugged frame had lived up to its advertising hype, and made its way safely back to Uttoxeter. Fortune was obviously smiling on Shwetz since, from whatever direction the emergency services were converging on Blithfield, he saw neither police car nor ambulance. The Range Rover was even now on a low loader, registration plates removed, and on its way to a crusher in a scrapyard run by a compatriot of Simonenko on the outskirts of Stoke-on-Trent.

Simonenko was amazed at how quickly this thing had spun out of control. His brain was in overdrive as he tried to discover some way of salvaging everything he'd worked for since he came to the UK. True, his money was safe enough – some in Switzerland, some in Luxembourg and the bulk in the Caymans – but what mattered now was his ability to make more, and he didn't want to start over yet again, not if he didn't have to.

The Range Rover wasn't a problem, even if someone had managed to take its number. It was Shwetz's personal vehicle, and he too was on his way to the crusher.

No, the problem was the business, all of whose records were on that wretched hard drive. Now that the fiasco at the reservoir had brought the police into play, he had to assume that the hard drive would inevitably find its way into their hands, and their forensic IT specialists would, sooner or later, unravel all its data.

Based on information supplied by contacts on the force, he suspected that backlog and heavy workload would combine to make that unravelling come later rather than sooner. That should give him time to develop a new strategy.

The other problem was the girl. Recovered from the Honda, she was now in a container parked in the yard at Uttoxeter.

But she couldn't stay there.

So was she any further use as leverage?

Probably not.

Time, then, to get rid of her.

Friday

25th April 2003

Newton Hall Dower House – 6:00 am

It was the first item on the early morning news.

The unidentified body of a young girl, aged around six or seven, had been found washed up on a beach on Foulness Island. She had been in the water less than twelve hours. It was far too soon for an autopsy to have been performed, but a reporter on site claimed to have information about the girl having been restrained and sexually assaulted prior to being dumped in the sea.

Shock and horror were evident in varying degrees on the faces of everyone gathered in the drawing room. The immediate silence was soon broken by murmured protestations of denial and disbelief, accentuated by a sleepless night spent anticipating the worst, yet hoping for the best.

At a writing desk against one wall sat a police constable with all the equipment needed for monitoring and recording incoming calls. On one of the two sofas in the room sat Detective Chief Superintendent David Fletcher and his assistant, DI Janet Harvey. The killing of an off-duty police officer who had only stopped to admire the view, linked to the abduction of a child belonging to one of the most important families in the county, required a police presence of significant seniority. As the news story played out on the TV screen, DCS Fletcher seemed to visibly deflate.

Richard sat slumped in one of several French upholstered armchairs set against the walls of the room. He had long since surrendered the hard drive to the police who had so far kept to themselves their collective opinion on the aborted exchange of hardware for Abby. Richard now seemed to have shrunk inside himself, as though unable to cope any longer with the furore his actions had unleashed.

Andy had been on his feet, pacing slowly up and down, continually blaming himself for not being able to prevent the Range Rover getting away. Occasionally, he would exchange words with his colleague Robert Cherville-Thomas – known to one and all as Cherry – until the news item stopped him dead in his tracks.

James was perched on the arm of the other sofa, where Bill Siddons sat huddled with his wife. They had all been gathered in this room ever since DCS Fletcher had turned up at Blithfield and escorted the party back to the Dower House, leaving the car park to the scrutiny of the scene-of-crime officers. Statements had been taken, recorded and signed, and then gone over again, and again. Richard's evidence had been rambling, disjointed and, at times, almost incoherent. It was clear that, on his own, the police would not have been inclined to take him seriously. In the end though, the fire and unexplained death at his computer shop together with Abby's abduction gave his story credence.

James was staring at the TV screen, ignoring everyone around him. One by one, faces turned towards him, most showing sympathy and compassion, but in a few these were tinged with curiosity as to how he might react. For several seconds he didn't react at all, but eventually years of training and discipline kicked his brain into gear and he leant forward, silently frowning, and slowly shaking his head.

Finally, he sat back, pursed his lips and looked over at Andy.

"This doesn't make any kind of sense," he said, gesturing at the TV. "Where would that poor kid need to have been dumped to wash up on Foulness?"

He looked around the room.

"Anyone?" he asked, but there was no response other than several head shakes.

"OK," he said. "But we're obviously talking about a boat, not a chopper or a plane. That reporter mentioned signs of restraint, not evidence of a fall from height."

"Yeah," broke in Andy. "But it's early days, James. That reporter probably hasn't a clue what he's talking about."

"Accept that," James replied. "But just think... ... If someone was wanting to... ... to dispose of my Abby... ..."

He paused as emotion threatened to overwhelm his thinking, and everyone waited patiently for him to continue.

Training, he thought. *Push it down. Deal with it later.*

"Abby," he said finally. "There are plenty of places and plenty of ways to dispose of a child's body before you get anywhere near the coast... ...And the guys on the boat clearly couldn't have cared less whether this child was washed up or not. This was not a clean disposal... ... so why go to the effort of a drive to the coast and a trip out to sea."

Again, he looked around the room, studying faces for reaction.

"Like I said," he concluded, "this doesn't make sense... ... That child is not Abby."

It was as though the room itself heaved a sigh of relief, and the atmosphere lightened ever so slightly.

DCS Fletcher was not entirely convinced, but was more than happy to go along for the present. He turned to DI Harvey.

"Get a photo of Abby down to Essex. Tell them I want a comparative ID immediately."

Harvey turned and nodded at her detective sergeant who had been hovering near the door. He acknowledged this with a nod of his own and turned to leave the room, reaching for his phone as he did so.

Newton Hall Dower House – 8:05 am

When the phone rang, James was sitting at the kitchen table nursing a steaming mug of Russian Caravan tea, dark and strong, no milk, no sugar.

He was enjoying a brief respite from the huddle of police personnel who had taken over his drawing room. They were waiting for the kidnapper to make his next call, which they all seemed certain would come sooner or later. James had consigned them, with all their equipment, to Andy's more than capable hands. His only companion at the moment was a tearful Mrs Siddons who was busying herself around the kitchen with chores that didn't need doing. Bill had taken himself down to the cellar, a large area lit by high windows at ground level, which Lady Helena had years ago divided into two rooms to serve as butler's pantry and wine cellar.

As he stared into his mug, James's thoughts were so far away that he didn't immediately notice the ringtone of his mobile phone. Mrs Siddons, on the other hand, gazed at it in horror as it buzzed and vibrated its way across the kitchen table. Eventually, its volume reached a pitch that penetrated the black shroud that had temporarily numbed his consciousness.

He reached out to take the phone from Mrs Siddons whose trembling hand had snatched it up just as it was about to plummet from the table's edge.

"Montrayne," he said.

"James, thank God," said a voice he recognised.

The Revd John Middlehurst had been a good friend to him after Sarah died, and not just because he was the pastor who had married them, and dedicated their only child. Their paths had first crossed in Northern Iraq in 1991. Revd Middlehurst was on his second overseas posting as a military chaplain and James had been a captain in the Royal Marines when 3 Commando was the spearhead force of Operation Safe Haven. They had served together again in Bosnia in 1995 when the padre had been completing his final tour as a military chaplain. They had both seen humanity behaving at its worst and, all too rarely, its best. Married to a girl who was a committed Christian, and with only a fledgling faith of his own, James had been intrigued by the padre's trust in a God who seemed conspicuously absent from the horrors to which they were both unwilling spectators. After the massacre at Srebrenica, a few tortuous, late-night conversations had formed a powerful bond between the two men.

"Hello, John," replied James. "Is it important? You've not picked the best time I'm afraid."

"Yes, I know, James. I know. I just wondered if there was any news of Abby."

James sat back in his chair, frowning.

"How do you know about that, John? There's supposed to be a police blackout."

DCS Fletcher had assured him, just before he left the house, that the lid was on tight and would stay that way until Abby was safely back home again.

"Ah... ..."

The hesitation told James that the reverend was trying hard not to get someone into trouble for speaking out of turn.

"Come on, John. Who've you been speaking to?"

"Well... ... Cathy Crockford saw your Omega being carted away by a tow truck... ... In a bit of a state, it was, apparently... ... She told us about it at the deacons' meeting last night. She'd seen Bill Siddons drive through the village earlier in the afternoon so after the meeting I phoned their cottage to check he was all right."

James glanced at his housekeeper who was watching him anxiously with red-rimmed eyes.

"And Mrs Siddons told you all about it, I suppose."

"James, she didn't plan to... ...She was very upset... ... just burst into tears, even though she told me Bill was OK. I couldn't work out what was wrong, until she mentioned Abby. Then it all came out... ... It was all too much for her, James. She just had to let it out."

Tears were once again tumbling down Mrs Siddons' cheeks.

"Hang on a minute, John," said James as he laid his phone down on the table.

Getting up from his chair, he walked around the table to where his housekeeper stood dejectedly watching him, arms dangling limply by her sides. Coming close, he reached out and gently drew her towards him. She almost collapsed onto his chest which, thankfully, was more than up to the task of supporting her. She was trying to speak, but her sobs made the words muffled and indistinct.

"It's OK, Doris," he said to the top of her head, breaking his own rule and addressing her by her Christian name.

"It's OK," he said again. "You've done nothing wrong. Don't worry about it."

She pulled back a little, sniffed, swallowed, and then managed to say, "But I am sorry. I should've known not to say anything... ... I should have known."

"There's no harm done," said James, hoping that was true. Then, still holding her, he moved slightly so that he could reach down to pick up his phone.

"John... ... You still there?"

"Yes, still here."

"Good... ... Now, have you told anyone else about this?"

"Not a soul, James. Mrs Siddons said that there was lots of activity up at the Dower House last night, so I thought it best to wait until this morning before giving you a call... ... I also hoped that you might have some good news by then."

He left the last sentence hanging, almost like a question, so James released Mrs Siddons and sat down, asking her to make them both another cup of tea, and told his friend the whole story.

"James," said the pastor as his friend finished speaking, "I really don't know what to say."

"Nothing you can say, John. It is what it is."

"I know, but... ... You know I'll be praying for you, and for Abby."

"Of course, John, and I appreciate it... ... ..."

He stopped, and the hesitation was not lost on the pastor.

"I think I sense a *but* in there, James."

He was right.

"Sorry, John... ... ... It's just... ... Well, if we're honest, we've both seen enough to know that things don't always work out well, no matter how much praying is done."

"I get what you're saying, James... ... and you're right, but I'll be praying anyway."

At that moment, there was the sound of hurried footsteps on the polished wooden boards of the rear hall.

"Thanks, John... ... Look, I'd better be going, and er... ... ... I'll let you know what happens."

The kitchen door opened, and the face of an unbelievably young police constable peered around it.

"Sorry, sir," he said, in a tone of respectful urgency. "Inspector Harvey needs you. It wasn't a phone call. It was an email."

Dakers Lodge, Staffordshire – 8:15 am

Bohdan Simonenko picked up his Sony Vaio PCG-SRX99 laptop and stood for a moment, looking around his library. As long as that laptop came with him, police forensics could spend a month in the house and come up with nothing that could link him to the disappearance of Abby Montrayne. Even if they turned up showing an unhealthy interest in his business affairs, the same applied. They would find nothing.

And they would come – eventually – though it would take some time. His registered address as Danny Simpkins was a Victorian, three-storey, detached house on the outskirts of Uttoxeter. Dakers Lodge was owned by a shell company based in the Bahamas with no traceable connection to Danny Simpkins, Bohdan Simonenko or Simpkins Logistics.

But sooner or later someone would talk: a guest perhaps, who had stayed at the house; or maybe they would find one of the girls he used.

Yes, the police would come. The only question was whether they would actually be able to charge him with anything. He'd leave his lawyers to handle that one.

His deep sigh was almost a snarl. He was still amazed at how quickly this business had unravelled. He promised himself that he would choose his subordinates with a great deal more care in future. Shwetz had come to him from someone he trusted, so now he would have to re-evaluate his scale of trust. He would probably come off OK this time, but he couldn't afford to be let down so badly again. In the meantime, while he was out of the country, it would be up to Geoff Mills over in Liverpool to manage the business. Mills was solid, dependable, with over twenty years' experience in the haulage industry. Simonenko knew Mills would keep things ticking over until it was safe for him to return. And if things did go belly up, Mills could take the heat.

Unfortunately, this was not the first time that circumstances and disloyal or incompetent subordinates – he never blamed himself – had conspired to necessitate a strategic withdrawal.

He walked through to the impressive entrance hall, whose marble floor set up a slight echo under his footsteps. He was annoyed at having to send his guests away early, and he didn't want to leave this impressive house, but a temporary absence was clearly a wise precaution as things stood.

Sending the email had been his last task before leaving, and he was absolutely certain that tracing it back to its source would prove impossible both for the police and for Montrayne's security people. If they accepted it at face value, it should buy him at least eight hours, a more than adequate safety margin when they didn't even know who they were looking for.

Everything else he would need for his trip was already packed into the boot of his Lexus GS430. Officially, if anyone should later be asking, this was a business trip to cement relations with a good customer in the United Arab Emirates. A few weeks of self-indulgence spent on his client's luxury motor-yacht would certainly be a fair recompense for having to leave the country in such a hurry. It was fortunate that he had to hand exactly the right sweetener to encourage his client to co-operate with his wishes.

He hoped that Rashid Bin Zayed Al Kasimi would appreciate the gift that was even now speeding towards him, crated up and ready for immediate use. He knew he'd been right not to transport the child himself. It was too long a journey, posing too many opportunities for things to go wrong. He would keep his distance until the last minute

Simonenko himself had no use for little girls. He liked them fully blossomed, but didn't mind them in their late teens as long as they were experienced enough to give him what he wanted. For some reason which he couldn't quite explain, he had always been slightly wary of men who needed to use children to satisfy their sexual urges. He didn't mind watching grown women performing, but whatever Al Kasimi had planned for the child, Simonenko hoped he'd do it with the cabin door closed.

Simonenko set the alarm and locked the front door. His few staff, none of whom lived on the premises, had already been given a fortnight's leave. There was nothing left to do but climb into the Lexus and head for Felixstowe.

Newton Hall Dower House – 8:55 am

The email had come with a video attached.

In spite of DI Harvey's assurances that it contained proof of life, nothing more or less, it had taken a huge exertion of will for James to force himself to watch the brief bit of footage.

In spite of his best efforts, he had not been able to prevent his eyes filling with tears at the sight of his little girl lying on the floor of a wooden crate with a copy of that morning's early edition clutched to her chest. The fear in her eyes had caused his stomach to twist itself in knots and, for a moment, there was the taste of bile in the back of his throat before a rage he'd seldom felt before took violent hold of him.

It had taken Andy, the detective sergeant and two constables to restrain him, but not before a marble bust of the Roman goddess Diana had been hurled through the drawing-room window like a cannonball to smash to glittering fragments on the path outside.

Just as quickly as it had erupted, the rage subsided, helped perhaps by Andy's laconic comment, "I do hope that wasn't the real thing."

As concerned hands slowly released him, James's eyes focussed on the computer screen again but the video had been turned off.

To show that he was fully in control of himself again, James turned to Andy and said, "No…… not real… … reproduction. The original sold at Sotheby's for… … oh, about eight million."

"Glad we got that settled," said his friend with a grim smile. "Now, do you think we can get back to business?"

They all turned as the door opened to reveal Mrs Siddons, quivering with apprehension.

"What's happened?" she asked in a voice they could barely hear.

James went over to her quickly and explained, begging her pardon for startling her so violently. Slightly calmer, she went away to make more tea, leaving James and the others to work out what to do in response to this latest message from the kidnapper.

Poseidon Moorings, River Orwell, Suffolk – 9:05 am

There were not many marinas on the East Coast with berths capable of accommodating the Desert Shroud II, which is why Rashid Bin Zayed Al Kasimi had decided to build his own. The project, to buy and convert a run-down marina on the River Orwell, had sounded rather grand when his local agent had applied to the planners some three years previously. As it turned out, it had actually involved little more than amalgamating the multiplicity of small berths into a couple of large ones capable of handling boats up to sixty metres with an eight foot draft. The premises on shore had proved to be unworthy of upgrading to the level of luxury appropriate to the status of the moorings' new owner. That had not deterred the Arab, however, as ideal premises had been discovered just a little way inland which would be most suitable for conversion to offer the luxurious seclusion he had in mind. That quiet isolation was to prove its worth today.

The Desert Shroud was a luxury motor-yacht measuring one hundred and sixty feet in length, and each foot had cost Al Kasimi a cool $125,000. Not that he'd been particularly troubled by the size of this expense. The income from his investments in Dubai had scarcely been dented by the purchase of his floating pleasure palace.

Al Kasimi had been furious when the child had died before he could fully exploit her tender innocence. It was such a waste to have to dump her small corpse overboard as they had left the English Channel behind and entered the North Sea. He had no idea why he was drawn so irresistibly towards little girls. It had always been that way, and he had never seen any good reason to resist the impulse. This did not mean that he could not perform adequately with a grown woman, but the hunger and the thrill were never the same as when he forced himself onto the luscious, uncharted territory of a young girl's body.

Only a very few people were aware of his inclinations, and he took great care to keep it that way. His crew could be trusted implicitly. Most of them had families in the UAE, all of whom were within reach of Al Kasimi's long, wealthy and powerful arms. In the UK, one person alone had discovered his sexual preferences, and that person had secrets of his own to hide.

Bohdan Simonenko had once become curious about the delivery instructions for an eight year old girl his agents had trafficked out of Eastern Europe. The ultimate destination seemed to correspond surprisingly closely with the holiday retreat of an Arab client of his freight forwarding business. In the belief that knowledge is power, he had tracked the package to its endpoint, and discovered that his suspicions were correct. He knew who owned the villa, and indeed the entire small Greek island which sheltered on the eastern side of Paxos in the Ionian Sea.

Simonenko had hoarded the information, just as he had other titbits which had come his way, against the time when it may prove useful. Never knowing just when that time might come, he kept track of his potential targets, ensuring that he knew where each one was at any given time.

Al Kasimi had no idea that his secret was known beyond a close, very tightly controlled circle until he received a phone call late the previous evening. He had been inclined at first to ignore the call since it was late and the name Danny Simpkins did not immediately register. However, when his steward informed him that the caller wanted to discuss a consignment delivered to his Greek island, he had cautiously agreed to take the call.

As soon as Simonenko had reminded him about the last cargo he had been contracted to ship out to Dubai, the penny had dropped. One does not easily forget a multi-million pound worth consignment of solid gold bathroom fittings intended for a new luxury hotel complex being developed in the fastest growing city in the UAE. It was quite fortuitous that Simpkins Logistics had been the freight forwarder of choice for the very select manufacturer of bespoke bathroom fittings situated close to Birmingham's Jewellery Quarter.

On hearing Simonenko's proposal, Al Kasimi's initial response had been simply to change his destination and head for a port on mainland Europe, where he could make plans to deal with this obvious threat to his security.

But that would mean passing up a very enticing offer.

A young unblemished girl from an English family of good breeding was being handed to him on a plate. And all in exchange for a safe, and wholly unobtrusive, passage out of the UK. It was more than the Arab could resist.

The deal had been struck and Al Kasimi slept late into the morning as he waited for his guest and his reward.

Newton Hall Dower House – 9:15 am

James was sitting on the settee which Bill and Mrs Siddons had occupied earlier. A coffee table, drawn up close to his knees, accommodated his laptop. Richard's problems, including that troublesome hard drive, had now been deposited squarely in the lap of the police, and James was content to leave them there. He now had something far more important to focus his attention on.

He was staring intently at the screen, reviewing the kidnapper's video, when the door opened and a young man, smartly dressed in sports jacket and slacks, came into the room. James looked up, slightly irritated, not wanting to be disturbed.

"I'm really sorry, James," said the young man, catching James's expression and interpreting it correctly. "I know you've got a lot on… … of course you have… … and I wouldn't disturb you… … but, you see, it's all arranged, and now I don't know what to do."

"*What* is all arranged, Ben?" James asked, restraining his impatience.

Ben Marshall was the nephew of the head gardener at the Dower House and, although he had a good degree in English Literature, he had been out of work since leaving university the previous year. Undeniably a conscientious young man, generally reliable and efficient, he had been helping on the estate in a voluntary capacity for several months when James suddenly found a new use for him. The plane crash which had wreaked havoc in the family such a short time ago had also bestowed on James new responsibilities which he had neither time nor inclination to manage efficiently himself. He needed a personal assistant.

Ben had jumped at the opportunity and, in the past fortnight, had fully justified James's confidence in him, but this business with Abby had shaken him as badly as anyone else.

"It's the interview, James," he said, and immediately saw that his boss hadn't the faintest idea what he was talking about.

"The Moving On programme," Ben persisted. "We arranged the interviews for the new CEO for this afternoon, but now... ..."

Moving On was one of several charities which James had set up using funds from his godmother's substantial bequest. As the Earl of Aullton, he now wished to rationalise the charities into one trust, The Aullton Trust, and the former CEO of Moving On was to become one of the managing trustees of the new trust. Consequently a replacement for him had to be found. The shortlist had been whittled down from five possibles to two very promising, and both candidates were due to have lunch with James at a restaurant in Lichfield at one o'clock, prior to interviews beginning at two thirty.

James shook his head.

"No way, Ben," he said. "Not today."

He sighed as his brain tried to deal with this new complication.

"You'll have to handle it yourself."

"Me!"

Ben was horrified, but James didn't really have time for this distraction.

"Either that, or postpone it. Get them to come back another time."

Having nothing more to say on the matter, James pushed the interviews from his mind and turned his attention back to the laptop. Ben hesitated for a moment, obviously unsure what his next step should be. Finally, recognising that his boss had more important things to be worrying about for the present, he turned for the door. James had told him to handle it, so that's exactly what he would do, though he hadn't quite decided how.

Scrutinizing the screen carefully, his emotions well in check now, James resisted the urge to gaze at his daughter's face.

IT had never been his strongpoint but developments in education had forced him to embrace the computer as a useful adjunct to his classroom. He had become proficient, though by no means expert. He had no idea what kind of camera had been used to record the video, but it was clear that the light had been focussed on Abby's face and the newspaper, so that the sides of the crate had faded to merge with a much darker background.

And it was the background on which James was now focussing his attention.

He had used the *Print Screen* function to isolate and save a section of the video and it was this still picture that now held him engrossed. Zooming in, and adjusting the brightness and contrast, he had been able to clarify some of the background detail. As he stared at the image, his mind grappling with the implications of what he saw, he wondered why the police had not decided to do this for themselves.

He looked over to where DI Harvey was speaking with the officer in charge of the monitoring equipment.

"Have you got anyone analysing this video?" he asked.

She finished whatever instruction she was giving to the constable, and turned towards him, her expression conveying both sadness and sympathy.

"No need really," she told him. "It gives us what we need... ... and want. It's a proof of life, nothing more, nothing less."

"Really?" replied James. "Then what would you make of this?"

Harvey came over to stand behind the settee so that she could look over his shoulder at the laptop screen. Andy, curious at this little exchange, came to stand beside her.

"What am I looking at?" asked the Inspector.

James had split the screen so that the full image could be seen on the left and the enlarged portion on the right. He pointed at something that looked like a pale smudge on the full image.

"OK," she said. "So what is it?"

"It's this," said James, pointing now at the enlarged image. "It's a label on one of the crates to the side of her."

Harvey turned to Andy, shaking her head sadly.

"It's nothing," she said quietly. "Probably just some junk in the room where they're keeping her. It could have been there for... ... who knows how long."

She rested her hands on the back of the settee and leant forward.

"Mr Montrayne, all we have to do is wait for the next phone call. We know your little girl is safe... ... That's what the video was telling us. Before long, we'll have the next demand, and then we can decide what to do... ... In the meantime, everything that can be done is already being done."

"And what is that exactly?" asked Andy.

Harvey sighed, but she knew this was a trying time for family and friends of a child victim, so she answered in a tone of quiet patience.

"We have search warrants for the haulage company's premises and for the home of Mykyta Shwetz. Officers are at both sites now and, believe me, they'll be tearing them apart... ... We've put an alert out for Shwetz, and other employees of the company are being interviewed as we speak. We don't know that the owner of the company is involved and without evidence we couldn't get a warrant for his place, but we do have a team watching the house, although... ..."

She frowned, "Neighbours say the house is occupied by a young couple who've been renting it for the best part of a year... ... They've never seen anyone answering to the description of Danny Simpkins."

James didn't appear to be listening, but Andy had followed every word. He pulled gently on the sleeve of Harvey's jacket to move her away from the settee.

"Didn't it occur to any of you that all this activity might just scare him into disposing of Abby and making a run for it?"

Harvey appeared to take no offence at the implied criticism.

"Believe me," she said. "I have done this before."

"Have you?" asked Andy. "Well, you can believe me when I tell you, so have I… … There are three types of child kidnap… … a parent denied custody or access runs away with their child – child in no real danger; then there's the sexual predator – child usually ends up dead; and finally, there's the kidnap for ransom – quite rare in this country these days, and the outcome could go either way… … Now, which of these have you done before?"

The inspector looked uncomfortable.

"Let me guess," he said. "The first… … family custody… … Am I right?"

She compressed her lips and gave no answer.

Andy stared at her for a moment, and then moved around the end of the settee to sit beside James.

Pulling out his mobile phone, he said, "Let me look at that again."

It took three phone calls, a certain amount of cajoling, a threat of police investigation, and a period of being put on hold, but at the end of fifteen minutes he had what he wanted.

He had set his mobile on speaker which had allowed Inspector Harvey both to confirm her identity and to follow every detail of the conversations. She was now looking sheepishly guilty.

"That label," said Andy, summing up what they'd just learnt, "is on a crate which is part of a shipment of porcelain which left Stoke-on-Trent yesterday afternoon en-route to Dubai. The reference number proves it… … And whatever container that shipment is in, so is Abby."

He looked at James.

"I'm sorry, my friend, but I don't think he intends to give her back at all. That video was just to buy himself some time."

James nodded slowly and then stood up. His expression of controlled rage caused Inspector Harvey to say, "I'll put out an alert for all Simpkins Logistics trucks... ... I must emphasise, Mr Montrayne... ... you have to let the police handle this."

James was already heading for the door.

"You handle it in your way, Inspector... ... but that's my little girl, so I'll handle it my way."

Cambridge Services, A14 – 10:05 am

Abby's tears had finally dried up some time during the night. Not that she had been aware that it was night. The darkness inside her box was absolute.

She tried blinking, and rubbed at her eyes, but it made no difference. Eyes open, eyes closed, there was nothing but blackness.

She didn't scream. It hadn't done any good before, and only made her throat sore.

She called for her daddy, and she called for Jesus, but nobody came. She wondered about that. Her daddy had told her that Jesus was always with her, but there was no sign of him in her box.

When it had all begun, she had been terrified. She had kicked, and screamed, and bitten, and cried, but she couldn't stop what was happening. And then she had become strangely woozy before falling into a nightmare-ridden sleep. At one point in her dreams, it had seemed as though she was being supported over a toilet by someone wearing a jacket whose hood was drawn tight around the face. One of the hood's drawstrings had dangled down in front of her and she had reached out to try and touch it only to see the head drift away from her and fade into darkness.

The next time she had woken, she had been inside the box and her terror had returned, creeping slowly into her blackness. The slow dawning of awareness had restrained the rising panic so that she had been able to think as she wept, gradually working out the nature of her surroundings. Only as the horror of her situation gradually settled into her consciousness did she start to claw at the wooden boards that confined her, screaming her fear and frustration to the uncaring darkness.

Eventually, drained and defeated, and strangely soothed by the low rumble that seemed to come from somewhere behind and beneath her, she had fallen into an exhausted sleep.

When she woke again, the rumble had stopped and she wondered what that meant, if it meant anything at all.

She blinked and rubbed at her eyes and felt around with fingers made sore by her efforts to escape. She had an idea that she had found holes in the top of the box, round holes that someone had made on purpose. She whimpered at the pain of her torn nails as she touched the boards just inches above her head.

And sure enough, there they were, a scattering of round holes rather bigger in diameter than her thumb.

She shifted awkwardly trying to get an eye to one of the holes, and when she finally managed it, she howled.

The space outside the box was as black as the inside.

She banged with her fists, and she kicked with her boots, all the time screaming as loudly as she could. Surely someone would hear. Surely her daddy would come and get her. Surely Jesus would save her.

And then the rumble started again and, after a moment, her box gave a very slight lurch.

She knew she was moving.

The box was taking her away from her daddy and she didn't know where she was going.

She called for him over and over again, but still he didn't come.

This time, the tears would not flow. Instead a strange numbness crept over her, beginning at her extremities and progressively seeping into the core of her being, like ice steadily claiming an animal lost in a freezing blizzard. Her mind gradually closed down, and her breathing slowed until she lay huddled on the floor of her crate, deathly still.

Newton Hall Dower House – 10:25 am

The helicopter settled gently onto the front lawn of the Dower House. Its rotors slowed and the howl of the twin Pratt & Whitney engines diminished to a subdued whine.

The AW109 Power was a highly versatile machine which had recently attracted the attention of James's father. The new Marquess of Thurvaston was determined to continue his work as head of the Defence/Trade Liaison Office based in London. His suddenly broadened responsibilities made fast and efficient transport a must. Only two weeks ago, James had accompanied his father to the East Midlands airport for a demonstration flight in this very aircraft. It was currently owned by a hedge-fund manager who was thinking of upgrading to the soon-to-be-available AW139. Never one to miss an opportunity, he ensured that whenever he was out of the country, as now, his helicopter was available for private charter.

The pilot, detecting no immediate urgency, decided to step down and stretch his legs, leaving the machine under the supervision of his trainee·co-pilot. He was barely out of the aircraft when he was confronted by two men, casually dressed and carrying large sports bags. He looked at them warily noting their hard, unfriendly expressions. If it wasn't for the fact that he knew he'd done nothing to warrant it, he might have thought they were both angry with him.

"Chuck these in here, shall we?" asked one, and they both tossed their bags onto the floor of the passenger cabin without waiting for an answer.

The pilot shrugged his unconcern. He wasn't interested in who they were or what was in the bags. He was paid good money to fly where he was told, and to do it smoothly and efficiently.

He knew neither of them was Lord Aullton since he remembered him and his father from their meeting two weeks previously. He didn't have time to wonder where his lordship was since the front door of the house opened and James Montrayne emerged with a harassed looking woman on his heels. Another man followed behind them carrying an obviously heavy bag over his shoulder.

The pilot watched, his interest piqued by the frustration evident in the woman's body language. As the trio grew closer, the pilot found he could hear what was being said over the low whine of the twin turbines.

"… … …can't just go charging off like this," the woman was saying.

"I most certainly can," Montrayne replied.

"But we're already doing everything we can," said the woman. "Going off like this isn't going to help."

"Inspector Harvey," said Montrayne, raising his voice to make sure he could be heard above the engines. "You may think that sitting around my drawing room counts as doing everything we can… … and maybe you're right. Maybe the police are doing as much as their limited resources will allow, but I'm not… … and I can't sit here while my little girl's in trouble… … So, I'm going to find her."

The woman reached out to grab his arm.

"You really need to leave this to the professionals."

Montrayne stopped and looked down at the hand clutching his sleeve. It was quickly withdrawn.

"Wasn't it professionals who built the Tay Rail Bridge, Inspector?" asked Montrayne. "And Chernobyl?"

"Don't forget the Titanic, Boss," said the man with the bag.

The pilot's normal disinterest had evaporated, and he was beginning to wonder exactly what they were going to find when he landed his party at Felixstowe, as he'd been directed.

"But you don't know where she is… … not exactly… … not yet," shouted the woman.

"That's why I'm going to find her."

While they'd been speaking, the man with the bag had slung it into the helicopter to join the two already there.

Montrayne nodded at the pilot who immediately climbed aboard to be followed by the three men who'd brought the bags. Ignoring the continued protests of the woman, Montrayne waved to a red-haired man standing in the doorway of his house, before joining the others in the helicopter.

Andy Graham waved back, and then reached for his phone. He was already speaking before the helicopter began to lift off the grass.

North of Cambridge Airport, A14 – 10:30 am

Vadim Hordiyenko had, at first, simply been curious, but now he was seriously worried.

He'd been surprised to spot Pete Wilson's tractor-trailer rig in the HGV parking area at Cambridge services. It had caught his eye because, unlike his own rig, Pete's vehicle was decked out in full Simpkins Logistics livery. He'd expected Pete to be well on his way down the M11 to Stansted by now, but he didn't mind joining up with his fellow driver for a coffee and a fag before they went their separate ways. Pete was one of several British drivers working for SLAFFI, but Vadim generally got on OK with him.

As he'd climbed back into the cab of his truck to resume his own journey to Felixstowe, Vadim had cast a glance over at Pete's rig. A police motorway patrol car had pulled to a stop in front of it, and two officers were climbing out. As far as Vadim could tell, Pete didn't appear particularly concerned as he waited, hands in pockets, to see what the officers wanted.

Probably just a vehicle safety inspection, but Vadim had good reason for getting his rig underway before the police turned their attention to him.

He was now travelling eastwards along the dual-carriageway at a steady fifty-eight miles per hour. The top of the M11 was behind him, and he had just finished skirting north on the A14 around the beautiful old city of Cambridge. Felixstowe lay some seventy miles ahead. Vadim smiled to himself. Two more hours should do it, and then he would be rid of this dangerous cargo.

And then his smile vanished.

He was approaching a long layby which could easily accommodate several trucks like his, but today most of the space was empty. What *was* there, though, made him shiver.

A rig similar to his own, though with a different container on the trailer, was hemmed in by two police patrol cars. Two vehicle safety checks within the space of half an hour might be unusual, but it was not exactly unheard of. But for both those checks to be targeting Simpkins Logistics vehicles had to be more than coincidence.

Cruising past at a steady speed, Vadim caught sight of fellow driver, Andrey Kulyk, being escorted to the rear of the trailer. Apart from a brief glance as he passed them, the police paid Vadim no attention. As far as he knew, there would be no problem with Andrey's vehicle. Simpkins Logistics might cut a few corners, but their trucks were generally maintained to a decent standard. And the shipment, if he remembered correctly, was a consignment of heat exchangers en route from Rugeley to the Czech Republic. Nothing, really, for the police to be interested in.

So why were they stopping Simpkins Logistics trucks?

Vadim suspected he knew, and thanked the god he didn't believe in that he was driving a hired rig, sporting a nondescript livery no-one would recognise.

Two hours, he told himself. Two hours and it would all be over.

AW 109 Power, somewhere above Leicester – 10:40 am

James had given up trying to speak to Andy on his cell phone. The signal kept breaking up. He was now speaking on the helicopter's integrated phone system which seemed to give better sound quality than his own landline. In its VIP configuration, soundproofing of the passenger cabin went a long way towards reducing the noise of the engines, but not so much that James was tempted to put the phone on speaker.

John, Nat and Cherry all had to wait patiently while they listened to one half of the conversation.

After several minutes, James put the phone down.

"OK, guys," he said. "Andy was right."

It was Cherry who asked the question that was in all their minds.

"So what are we looking for, Boss?"

James, whose seat was facing forward, glanced over Cherry's shoulder into the cockpit. Both pilot and co-pilot were wearing headsets and seemed entirely focussed on what they were doing.

"We know that the truck that picked up the shipment from the pottery yesterday was a Simpkins truck. No question. That blue and yellow livery echoes the Ukrainian flag. Simonenko's little joke, maybe. Or maybe he's proud of his country."

"Unlikely," said Nat. "I thought they kicked him out."

"Whatever," replied James. "Thing is, they switched trucks this morning. Andy's been checking with other local hauliers, and he found a guy that helps Simpkins out when they get overbooked… … and vice-versa of course… … Anyway, this guy lent Simpkins a tractor rig. No trailer needed since they already had that loaded up with the container of porcelain. He sent it over to Simpkins at seven fifteen this morning."

"How do we know this is the rig we're looking for?" asked Cherry. "He could have used it for anything."

"We know because, when Andy asked them, the police confirmed that when they went to the yard with their search warrants there were three spare rigs in Simpkins livery just sitting there… … He didn't need to borrow one unless it was for camouflage."

Slowly, the other three nodded their agreement with his logic.

"So," said Cherry. "Back to my question… … What are we looking for?"

James looked down at a note he'd scribbled on a pad.

"According to the guy at Pilling Haulage, it's a Volvo FH12 6X2 420 TSC… … whatever that means. Anyway, it's a new tractor… … spotless, he says… … in Connaught green with a yellow lightning flash on each side."

John was about to speak, but Cherry beat him to it.

"And what about the container?"

James looked at his notes again.

"Andy says the guy at the pottery described it as a sort of rusty red."

While they were thinking about that, John got his own question in.

"Is this the only Pilling truck on the A14? If we find it, how can we be certain we've got the right one?"

"There are a couple of others," admitted James. "But we should be able to tell them apart... ... One of them is a curtain-sider, not a container... ... so, easy to rule that one out... ... The other is hauling a container, but it's blue with big white stars on each side. Again, should be easy to spot and rule out."

The others nodded, and James looked at each one for more questions. He welcomed questions, always had. It helped to make sure he didn't overlook anything.

This time it was Nat.

"Don't really like to mention this, but I suppose I should... ... What if the crate... ... the one Abby's in... ... what if it's already been taken out of the container? What if we're chasing the lorry, and she's not in it anymore?"

John glanced at Nat and it was clear he'd been thinking the same thing.

"Yeah, it's OK, Nat," said James. "I did wonder briefly about that myself, but I just don't see it."

"You'd better be right, Boss," said Cherry.

"I know," James replied. "But just think about it... ... If whoever's got her intended to keep her somewhere else... ... or dispose of her... ... why on earth put her in that container of porcelain in the first place?... ... There had to be a reason, and someone went to a lot of trouble to disguise that rig, so I think it's going all the way to Felixstowe... ... and I think Abby's in it."

They all nodded, hoping he was right, but then Nat spoke up again.

"Sorry to keep playing devil's advocate, Boss, but there's no point loading that container on board ship with Abby still in it. She'd be dead before it gets to wherever it's going."

He shrugged ruefully.

"Sorry, Boss."

"No, no... ... You're right, Nat. That's why we've got to find it as soon as we can... ... Look, we all know... ... in some weird, perverted circles, young girls are big money. According to Andy, my Abby could be worth a hundred grand to the right buyer... ... maybe even more to certain people... ..."

He paused and took a deep breath while the other three watched him, trying to imagine but barely comprehending the pain he was suffering.

"We'll find her, Boss," said Cherry eventually. "Count on it."

Newton Hall Dower House – 10:45 am

Andy preferred to make his phone calls out of earshot of the police which is why, for the past half-hour, he'd been out in the garden.

Returning to the drawing room, it needed little more than a glance to take in the scene of weary inactivity. Since there had been nothing from the kidnapper for over two and a half hours, the constable overseeing the monitoring equipment had nothing to monitor. Inspector Harvey was sitting on a settee staring into the mug of coffee on the table in front of her and wracking her brains trying to discover whether there was anything else she could have done but hadn't. Unable to think of any more orders to issue, she was virtually twiddling her thumbs. Her sergeant was standing by the window, nursing his own mug of coffee, and trying hard not to imagine what was happening to the child who had once played in those gardens.

Andy wasn't really interested in the police officers. It was Richard he wanted, but he thought he might as well ask, just in case.

79

"Anything?" he said to the inspector as he paused by her settee.

She looked up, frustration and anxiety showing in her eyes.

"Nothing yet from the searches of the premises... ... There have been a couple of trucks stopped and searched, but... ... negative again."

Andy nodded and went over to where Richard sat slumped in his chair by the wall.

"Come on you," he said. "Do you good to stretch your legs... ... and you must be needing a pee by now."

There was no response, so Andy kicked the boy's feet, not hard, but firmly enough to make him stir.

"On your feet," he said, reaching down to grasp Richard's arm and haul him off his chair.

The inspector sat up, looking as though she might be about to protest, but when Richard raised no objection and trotted meekly towards the door, she sank back into the cushions.

Her eyes narrowed slightly when she saw Andy pick up a laptop before following him, and her curious gaze followed the pair out of the room.

Once in the mural hall which connected the front and rear entrances, Andy pushed Richard in the direction of the cloakroom off the front end of the hall. After giving him time to do his business, he ushered him through to the library which was about as far away from the drawing room as it was possible to get without going upstairs or outside.

With Richard seated at a desk and the laptop open in front of him, Andy told him, "You need to look at those encrypted files again."

The boy stared blankly at the screen.

"Why?" he asked. "The police have the hard drive, and the decryption key... ... What d'you need me for?"

Andy sighed, and wondered whether slapping him around might provoke a more helpful response. Probably not. The boy's behaviour and moods seemed unpredictable, as though he wasn't functioning normally.

"Look, I saw you dump the contents of the hard drive onto this laptop before you gave it to the police. Ditto the decryption key... ... You couldn't help yourself. Backing up is second nature to you... ... plus, you couldn't bear to let them go.... ... Now, I need you to look through the records for any drops... ... deliveries... ... contacts between here and Felixstowe. Anywhere trucks have stopped in the past... ... Not legitimate deliveries. Just the dodgy stuff."

Richard stared up at him for a moment and then the blankness seemed to disappear. It was as though life began to stir behind his eyes. This was something he could do.

"I need that info fast," said Andy, noticing the change.

Richard nodded, his fingers already dancing over the keyboard.

AW 109 Power, somewhere North of Newmarket – 11:10 am

Mike Colman had been flying helicopters for most of his adult life. In the British Army Air Corps, he had started on the Westland Gazelle, before graduating to the Lynx in time for the war in the Balkans. Although he had trained for the new Apache attack helicopter due to be introduced in 2001, he never got the chance to fly it in action. An argument with a fellow chopper pilot from the RAF, the year after the three services had been brought under the one Joint Helicopter Command in 1999, had developed into a bloody brawl which his CO at Colchester had been unable to ignore.

Impatient with the new command structure, Colman had decided to resign his commission and try his luck in the growing civilian market. Reluctantly, his CO had accepted the loss of one of his best pilots, and no disciplinary action found its way into Colman's record.

Civilian flying paid well, and was probably more interesting than being a bus driver, though sometimes Colman doubted it. This particular assignment, however, intrigued him. At first he had thought it was to be a straightforward flight from a posh house near Uttoxeter to the port of Felixstowe, hardly worth

81

bringing a co-pilot along except to give Charley a chance to build up her hours.

Now, in the light of what he'd just been told, it looked like he and Charley were to be key players in foiling a kidnap plot.

Charlotte Emerson had over four hundred and fifty hours under her belt, and already possessed her commercial licence. She was currently building up her hours and experience, and wasn't far short of obtaining her cherished instrument rating. She might be the daughter of his boss, but Colman liked her. She was bright, conscientious and had a wicked sense of fun. She knew her ambition to succeed as a commercial helicopter pilot required dedication and hard work, but she wasn't afraid of either.

"I've always wanted to land one of these on top of a truck doing sixty miles an hour," she told Colman.

"Yeah, right," he replied. "Let's just hope, for the sake of your licence, it doesn't come to that."

She chuckled briefly, and then he heard a serious note creep into her voice.

"If it's the only way to save that little kid, Mike, I'd willingly toss the licence."

"Would you?" he asked. "Really?"

"Well, maybe not willingly... ... but, yes I mean it."

There was silence for a moment, as both of them considered the many CAA regulations that might have to be bent if they were to achieve their goal. James Montrayne had told them that they would both be well compensated for any financial loss arising out of today's exploit, but this wasn't just about money. For both of them, flying was their life; not something to be surrendered lightly.

"OK, Charley," said Colman eventually. "Let's get on with it. You'd best break the news to his Lordship."

James picked up the phone when it rang through from the cockpit. He listened, and began to frown as he took in the bad news.

Kentford, A14 – 11:15 am

It was PC Brian Moseley who first spotted the truck heading east on the A14. With lights and siren off, he closed the distance so that his partner, PC Sharon Milburn, could check the truck's details against the information they'd been given. As their blue and yellow chequered Volvo V70 crept alongside in the outside lane, Sharon could clearly make out the distinctive colour scheme of the tractor hauling the trailer rig.

"OK, Bri," she said, reaching for her radio. "We'd better stop him."

Moseley was an experienced driver who'd done this sort of thing many times before, but he was always vaguely aware that, weight for weight, his vehicle was no match for the thirty-eight tonne monster alongside him.

"Let's hope he decides to cooperate," was his only comment as he eased alongside the tractor cab.

"There's a layby coming up," said Sharon. "Let's give it a try."

Moseley flicked on his lights and blipped his siren to attract the driver's attention. Sharon lowered her window and pointed up at the driver who was now glancing anxiously down at her. Then she jabbed her finger forwards before curving it over to the left. She repeated the gesture and the driver nodded to show he understood.

"OK," she said to Moseley. "I think we're on the same page."

The Volvo pulled ahead of the truck and led, lights still flashing, for about a quarter mile before braking to lead off into the layby. Watching in his rear-view mirror, Moseley noted that the truck was following. Still braking, and thankful that the layby was empty apart from them, Moseley didn't notice that the truck was not braking. If anything, it was picking up speed.

"Bri!"

He heard his partner yell from beside him and, when he now looked in his mirror, he saw the truck powering down on them only yards to the rear.

His foot came off the brake just as the truck, half way over the hatching that separated the layby from the main carriageway, struck the right rear corner of his Volvo. The force of the impact flung the car forwards and both officers became momentarily trapped as their airbags deployed. The angle of impact caused the police car to twist sideways and its nose became entangled in the wood-and-wire fence that separated the layby from the field beyond.

The truck was picking up speed and, too late, the driver noticed that the nearside lane of the A14 was occupied by a line of heavy vehicles. These couldn't move over to the outside lane because of vehicles overtaking them, which left him with no space to pull out onto the carriageway. In desperation, he stabbed at his brakes.

The trailer disapproved of the sudden deceleration and its rear began to swing out onto the carriageway in the beginning of every truck driver's nightmare, the jack-knife. The first truck in the line was a fuel-tanker and, although it was already slowing, there was no way the driver could avoid the trailer swinging into his path. The point of collision, the speed of the truck, and the angle of impact all contributed to what happened next.

The trailer began to tip as the force of the tanker's impact shoved it sideways. Very slowly, the container began to topple. The tanker driver didn't see any more as his attention was grabbed by a jolt in the rear when he was struck by the truck behind which had been following too close for comfort.

As soon as he could safely manage it, the tanker driver pulled to a stop, climbed down from his cab raced back. The scene that confronted him was a mess. The container had slid from the trailer and landed on the roof of the police car, partially crushing it. There was no sign of movement inside. Nor was there any immediate sign of the driver of the truck that had caused all this havoc.

In anguished impotence, the tanker driver lifted his gaze from the smashed police car, and his eyes settled on a figure racing through a field of sugar beet.

Aware that there were others now gathering at the scene, hopefully better qualified than he was to deal with any injured, the tanker driver leapt over the smashed fence and set off in pursuit.

AW 109 Power, somewhere above Kentford – 11:20 am

James looked in turn at the faces anxiously watching him.

"According to our pilot, if the truck left Uttoxeter as early as we think it could have done, we may not catch up with it before Ipswich."

There was a concerted groan from the others.

"That's going to be cutting it fine, Boss," said Cherry, echoing the thoughts of them all.

"True... ... but that's not all," James told them. "Of course, we've got no idea whether he's taken any breaks, and how long they might have been if he did... ... So we need to start looking out for the truck from now onwards... ... Chances are we won't spot it before Stowmarket, but we've got to be looking."

Nat and John reached in their bags for powerful binoculars. John's were Canon 15 x 50, whereas Nat favoured Leica 10 x 42, and both were good enough for the task in hand.

"Listen up, guys," said James. "Our pilots have got clearance to take us on a flightpath north of the A14 for most of the way."

"What do you mean... ... most, Boss?" asked Cherry.

"There's a NOTAM advising a temporary airspace restriction over Stowmarket. We're going to have to go around it, which will mean losing sight of the A14."

"Shit!" exclaimed Cherry. "What the hell's going on?"

"Who knows," replied James. "Could be anything from a foreign head of state to hot-air balloons... ... keep watching while I talk to Andy."

He was still on the phone when there was an exclamation from Nat.

"Hell's bloody teeth! Would you look at that?"

Traffic on the A14 eastwards was at a standstill. The chopper was just coming up to the tail end of still moving traffic, but up ahead was chaos.

Colman slowed their progress so they could take in every detail of the scene. The rear of a police car could be seen jutting out from under the green container which had toppled from the trailer of a Simpkins Logistics truck.

"That's odd," said John.

"What is?" asked Nat.

"You wouldn't normally expect container doors to burst open like that," John told him. "They're usually sealed up tighter than a duck's arse."

But the doors of this container had sprung open and a number of cardboard cartons lay strewn about. Some of them had themselves burst open to disgorge their contents onto the surface of the layby.

"What are those brown things?" asked Cherry.

Nat and John were scanning the scene with their binoculars.

"Looks like handbags," Nat told him.

John was reading the stencilling on the boxes.

"Givenchy, Jimmy Choo, Prada… … D'you know what? I bet they're all knock-offs."

Meanwhile, Cherry had turned his attention to the windows on the other side of the cabin, where two running figures had caught his attention.

"Hey, take a look at this, guys," he said, nudging James to attract his attention.

Two men were running as best they could across a huge field of sugar beet. The second was clearly the fitter of the two and, as they watched, he closed the gap to the point where a diving rugby tackle was all that was needed to send the pair sprawling into the leaves of the beet.

The helicopter was moving away from the scene now, leaving all on board still unclear as to exactly what had happened. There was no point in hanging around though. It was undoubtedly tragic, but there was nothing they could do here, and much to be done elsewhere.

As they left the scene behind them, James looked back and spoke hesitantly, his voice taught with anger and sadness.

"One of you asked me… … some time back… …why I didn't tell the police about the truck we're looking for… … That's the reason… … I don't trust them to do it right."

East of the Orwell Crossing – 11:31 am

Dougie Frazer drove out of Ipswich on the Nacton Road to its junction with the A14 a few miles east of the Orwell Crossing Bridge. It had just been everyone's good fortune that he'd been at home doing a spot of decorating when he took the call from Andy Graham.

A few years ago, Dougie had been based with 16 Air Assault Brigade at their Colchester headquarters, until a damaged right knee had nudged him into retirement. A brief survey of potential employers had brought him to a medium-sized and well-respected security firm whose expansion and prestige was inextricably linked with the ever-growing Port of Felixstowe. Experience, sound judgement and a modicum of good luck had brought Dougie to the point where he now ran the company for the benefit of its only shareholder, an aging former paratrooper who seemed to like nothing more than standing in the middle of an Icelandic river with a fishing rod in his hand.

Dougie had never served with Andy Graham, but business had brought them into contact a time or two. As ex-servicemen, at the same level of management, in the same line of work, they had hit it off, and made use of each other's skills whenever necessary.

From all the information available to him, Dougie knew that, at this spot on the A14, he had to be ahead of the vehicle he was looking for. If it left the A14 at this point, as he'd been told was likely, it would drive right past where he was parked up on the grass verge. From this spot, he also had a clear view of the bridge where the A14 passed over the Acton Bridge Road. A

Pilling Haulage tractor-trailer rig, green cab with yellow lightning flashes, hauling a rust-red container was not going to get past him unobserved. To be sure, he had called in support.

Young Tommy Nettles, whose nickname inevitably was "Sting", was cruising along the westbound carriageway of the A14 while his boss lay parked up at the intersection. Sting also knew what he was looking for and, being fairly new in the job, was desperate not to let his boss down. Nor did he want to disappoint his uncle who owned the business, which relationship accounted for the fact that a comparative youngster with little experience had a job there in the first place. A wicked fast bowler, and captain of his university cricket team in his final year, he had been offered a place on the county team. Unfortunately for cricket nothing would do for young Sting but to join the family business. County cricket would not, he believed, afford the excitement he craved.

He had no real idea of what was going on, but the urgent call from Dougie had suggested something unusual was underway. Sting liked unusual. It sounded promising, and he wondered what could be aboard the truck that he was watching out for. The trouble was, he had no discretion to do anything on his own account. He simply had to report any sighting to Dougie who was in contact with someone in a helicopter.

If the timings were right, it was most unlikely he'd catch sight of the truck before he reached the A137 on the west side of the River Orwell. At this point, sighting or not, he was to divert to Whitfield Park, a country-club hotel with helicopter landing facilities. Here he would pick up four passengers, who could easily be accommodated in his pride and joy, a Mercedes 600 V12. True, the car was ten years old, but he kept it immaculate, as had the single owner before him. With his passengers aboard, he would then retrace his steps to Nacton.

After that, he had no idea, but he thought that the prospect must hold some possibility of excitement, something which his hormones and machismo craved.

He hadn't yet acquired the experience that would have told him that this was the sort of craving that could get you into trouble.

AW 109 Power, approaching Orwell Crossing – 11:32 am

They still hadn't spotted the truck when they had to divert away from the A14 to avoid the restricted airspace, but it no longer seemed to matter.

James had been sure that Abby would be removed from the container before the truck entered the Port of Felixstowe, but the question had always been… … where? Andy had got Richard searching Simonenko's files for possibilities, but what he'd actually come up with was pure gold.

Andy and Richard at the Dower House, and Rod still slaving away in his office at RRISC, had together discovered three significant facts. An Arab called Rashid Bin Zayed Al Kasimi owned an island off the coast of Greece to which Simonenko had once delivered a consignment described in his files as *Moldovan ~ 9 yrs ~ female ~ unblemished.* The same Rashid Bin Zayed Al Kasimi also owned an exclusive property called Poseidon Moorings on the River Orwell, a little east of the bridge. Al Kasimi's luxury yacht was even now occupying one of the two berths at the moorings.

Everyone was now convinced that this was where the end-game would be played out.

But for that they needed to be down on the ground, and here both Andy and Mike Colman had proved their worth. Swooping in by helicopter would certainly be the fastest approach, but it would hardly be unobtrusive. Something else was needed, and James was assured that this would be waiting for them as soon as they touched down at Whitfield Park.

Whitfield Park Country Club – 11:38 am

Tommy was watching the helicopter lift into the air when James, now occupying the seat beside him, nudged him gently in the side.

"We waiting for something?" James asked him.

Tommy looked startled, shook his head, and set the car in motion.

"Know where you're going?" asked James, as the big car eased over the speed bumps in the drive of Whitfield Park Country Club.

Tommy nodded.

"Back to the A14 and then east to the Nacton turn."

"That'll do," James told him and reached for his phone as it started to ring.

He did more listening than talking which allowed Tommy to hone in on the sounds coming from behind his seat. He'd seen enough of the right sort of movies to recognise the snaps and clicks for what they were. Once or twice, he risked a quick glance over his shoulder trying to catch a glimpse of weapons being prepared but, when his eyes caught those of James who paused in mid-sentence, he decided to dump his curiosity and just get on with doing what he was told.

When James put his phone away, his face broke into a grim smile of satisfaction.

"Mike, God bless him, has just spotted the truck. He says if we give it a couple of minutes we should pull onto the A14 right behind it."

"He sure, Boss?" asked Cherry, from his position in the centre of the rear seat.

"No question," James told him. "But there is something he's not so sure about... ... There's a grey Lexus... ... seems to be keeping pace with the truck. His co-pilot put the binos on it and she thinks it could be a GS430, but there's no way they can get close enough to say for sure... ... Plenty of other cars are passing the pair of them, and people with a Lexus don't normally tool along at fifty-five."

"Could be grandma and granddad out enjoying the views," suggested John from behind Tommy.

"Maybe… … but let's watch out for it," replied James.

And they did.

They found them, just as Mike had said; Lexus and Pilling truck travelling in tandem, east over the Orwell Bridge.

"So how are we going to do this, Boss?" asked Cherry, as Tommy took up position three vehicles back from the Lexus. It wasn't ideal because one of the vehicles was a huge, orange, Sainsbury's tractor-trailer rig which completely obscured their view directly ahead unless Tommy drifted into the outside lane which, all agreed, was not a good idea. Mike offered to try and keep them all in sight, but James told him to pull back and wait for them at Whitfield Park. He didn't want to have the truck driver, or whoever was in the Lexus, worrying about a suspicious helicopter hovering in the vicinity. They might think it meant that the police were closing in.

"We'll let him make the turn and see if the Lexus follows," said James. "If it does, at least we'll have a better idea what we're dealing with."

He turned his gaze on Tommy, and watched him for a few seconds.

"Tommy," he said. "I don't know what you've been told, but… … these guys we're following have got my little girl. She's in a crate… … in that truck. The police are looking in all the wrong places, so we're here to get her back. We're ready to do whatever it takes… … which means things could get a little messy. So when we meet up with Dougie, it might be best if you stay with him, and let us borrow your car for as long as it takes."

Tommy pursed his lips and stared straight ahead. He cringed at the thought of handing over his pride and joy to a set of complete strangers who would have no hesitation about taking her into the middle of something "messy".

He glanced at James.

"Your little girl," he said, statement not question.

James nodded.

"How old?"

"Almost six," James told him.

"Shit!"

Acton Bridge Farm – 12:05 pm

The earliest brick buildings had probably gone up when the first Queen Elizabeth was on the throne, but there had been many later additions as the farm had grown in size and prosperity. Sadly, two World Wars, an unfortunate marriage, a history of bad management, and EU regulations had all contributed to the farm's decline in success and affluence. During the post-war years most of the land had been sold until only a few acres and the vacant farm buildings remained. While not exactly derelict, the buildings were in a poor state of repair, and as such were ripe for sympathetic restoration and conversion.

Through an agent, Al Kasimi had made an offer for the property conditional upon planning permission being obtained for the style of conversion he had in mind. The core of the E-shaped, old farmhouse was definitely Tudor. He liked that and planned to keep it, and probably the Stuart and Georgian wings as well. The barns and other outbuildings would probably provide a swimming pool and other recreational facilities. As for the substantial yard, surrounded on three sides by the house and barns, he hadn't yet made his mind up about that. But today, it would provide the ideal turning space for the truck he'd been told to expect.

The yard also benefitted from a number of vantage points, high up in both the house and the barns, giving a clear view down into the open space. The building forming the left side of the yard, when viewed from the farmhouse, appeared to have been devoted to vehicle storage, judging by various ancient ploughing implements to be found at one end. The only vehicle it housed today behind its large, weathered doors was a shiny, black BMW X3, the vehicle used by Al Kasimi to travel the short distance up from the Desert Shroud.

And he hadn't come alone.

At a window on the upper floor of the house, the Desert Shroud's mate, or First Officer as he liked to call himself, knelt on the old carpet, cradling an H&K MP7. Panagiotis Gianopoulos had been with Al Kasimi for almost five years, the same as Desert Shroud's captain, Miltiades Petrides. Gianopoulos has earned his nickname of "Panny" not so much because of his name, but because of his method of disposing of his master's cast-offs. He would thrust their head in the toilet pan, and repeatedly press the flush until they stopped struggling. It never required much effort. Few were over ten years old.

He liked the MP7, partly because it was shorter and lighter than the MP5, with a greater effective firing range. He didn't particularly want to fire it today. He'd given it a thorough strip and clean the night before. On the other hand, if shooting someone was what was required, he had no objections.

He watched the yard, scratched his backside, and waited.

Al Kasimi was downstairs, looking through the window of what had once been the sitting room. He had keys to the house and other buildings, courtesy of the owner who was desperate to take advantage of the generous offer made for his property. Al Kasimi had no reason to expect trouble today, but he always liked to be ready for it.

And ready he most certainly was.

Samar and Aamir formed Al Kasimi's personal protection detail. They had been with him since they were boys in their teens, shaped and honed to his exacting standards. Now in their late twenties, they were intensely loyal, and fearfully protective of the golden goose that rewarded them so liberally.

Keeping company with the BMW, Samar looked across the yard to where Aamir was concealed in what had once, perhaps, been a hayloft. The only indication of his friend's presence was the occasional shadow which flitted across one of the narrow, vertical, unpaned slits which provided ventilation for the barn. Both carried Glock 19s in belt holsters, but today they were relying more on their H&K MP5Ks which both of them professed to prefer to Panny's MP7.

As Al Kasimi lifted his phone to his ear, he took another careful look around the yard. Sunlight dancing on decaying brickwork, gave it an air of quaint tranquillity. Not a threat in sight. Just as it should be.

Acton Bridge Road – 12:05 pm

The truck made the turn, leaving the A14 to head south on the Acton Bridge Road. Dougie watched it go, and saw the Lexus follow about twenty yards behind. He was on his phone to James when Tommy's Merc glided into his rear-view mirror. A moment later, James eased his bulk into the passenger seat beside him. The two men shook hands.

"Thanks," said James.

"No problem," Dougie told him. "Maybe I'll need a favour from you one day."

Two minutes later, James was out of Dougie's car and back in the Merc. Tommy had reluctantly joined Dougie in his Jeep Cherokee, having surrendered his driving seat to Cherry.

"They with us?" asked Cherry.

"No," said James. "They didn't like it, but they've done their bit. This is up to us."

He opened out the OS map that Dougie had given him, and folded it to show Ipswich and the Orwell Estuary.

"He's a good lad, that Dougie," he announced to the car in general. "While he's been sitting there, he's been using his brain... ... and his phone."

He held up the map so that, with John and Nat sitting forward and craning their necks, everyone could see.

"Here's us."

His finger stabbed at the map.

"And here's the moorings where this guy Al Kasimi's moored his boat. Dougie says there's no way that truck can make it all the way down, but the road's good enough as far as this farm here."

"Will it be able to turn round?" asked John from the back.

"It's a farm, John. There must be a yard... ... and some of these farm vehicles these days aren't minis."

"OK," John replied. "So, who lives at the farm? Do we know?"

"Dougie says it's derelict... ... not exactly falling down, but abandoned. While he was waiting for us, he called in a favour from some contact in County Hall and it seems Al Kasimi's put in an offer on the farm pending planning permission."

There was a collective sigh of relief in the car.

"So no-one else to worry about," said Cherry, voicing something which had been of concern to all of them.

"Just keep an eye out for walkers," said James. "According to this, there are no official public paths or bridleways close by, but you can never tell where folk will choose to walk these days."

He turned in his seat so he could look at each one of them.

"We ready for this?"

"You bet, Boss," came Cherry's affirmative, followed by nods from John and Nat.

"Right," said James, attention back on the map.

"We'll take the Merc as far as here. The road bends by these trees, and it looks like there's either a wide verge or a field entrance... ... After that, I'll follow the road keeping to the trees as far as the farm... ... Cherry, you take the field side of the road, keeping close in to the hedge... ... John and Nat, I want you to swing wide around this field, keeping the hedge between you and the farm buildings so you come up on the farm from the rear... ... If this map's right, the house is not joined on to the other buildings, so you'll have access to the yard if need be... ... Questions?"

There was a moment's pause for thought, then Cherry spoke.

"Clear enough, Boss, except maybe for one thing."

He glanced at the two in the back of the car as he spoke.

"Rules of engagement," said Nat.

"I'm not that bothered one way or the other," went on Cherry, "but... ... what exactly do you want us to do with these guys?"

James looked at each in turn. He had no wish for any of them to land up in serious trouble with the law. Revenge wasn't the issue. Getting Abby back safely was what counted.

"Don't take risks," he said. "Do what you have to do to keep safe and protect Abby. As for the rest... ... that depends on them. If we have some tidying up to do later, so be it. Nobody asked them to kidnap my daughter."

"Fine by me, Boss," said Cherry.

Nat and John both nodded.

John was rummaging in his holdall.

"Might be a bit chancy relying on phone signals out here," he said. "So I brought these along."

He took out four pocket-sized radios and some smaller gadgets.

"Bluetooth earpieces," he explained. "Everything's all charged up and ready to go. Range is good enough for anything we're likely to need. All set to Channel 1. If anyone's compromised, switch to Channel 5."

"Good lad," said Cherry. "Thanks."

He took radios for himself and James, and sat back as the car began to move off.

"Can't let them get too far ahead," said James. "We don't want that truck turning round and meeting us on the way out."

The other three began checking their weapons.

Acton Bridge Farm – 12:20 pm

Having climbed down from his cab and taken a good look around, Vadim decided to reverse his trailer into the farmyard. The swing would be wide and push his tractor unit onto the grass verge, but the ground seemed firm enough to take the weight.

The road passing the farm had a narrow, single-track, tarmacked surface, and had not been easy for him to negotiate from the point where it had left the Acton Bridge Road and become a designated Private Road. He had been cheered by the earlier reassurance from his boss, following in the Lexus, that there would be no chance of meeting anything coming the other way. With trees on one side, and hedge on the other, passing would have been impossible.

His boss, Bohdan Simonenko, was watching him now, having left his Lexus parked in the road just before the farmyard entrance. Beside him, standing in front of the open farmhouse door, was another man Vadim did not know. He looked foreign, maybe Middle-Eastern, Vadim thought, and he must be the guy who'd been waiting for this consignment. The two appeared to be talking amicably, and no weapons were in view.

He could see them both in his rear-view mirror as he eased the trailer far enough into the yard to give him a good angle for turning out again into the road.

There was no-one else in sight, but Vadim knew this business well enough to be sure there would be others nearby. He was equally sure that's where the weapons would be. He shivered, glad that they needed him to deliver this container to the Port of Felixstowe, otherwise… …

* * * * *

James was almost level with the rear of the Lexus. He was as sure as he could be that the car was empty, but he couldn't move any closer to find out without risking being spotted by the driver of the truck.

He waited, partly for confirmation that everyone else was in position, and partly because the truck was still moving. It might actually move out of sight altogether. He wasn't sure just how big the farmyard was. On the other hand, it might stop and the driver could climb down from the cab and walk into the yard, out of view.

Which is exactly what happened.

"Sitrep, guys, two, three, four," said James softly into his radio. The numbers had been allocated according to the anti-clockwise positions each would take up around the yard.

"Two," said Cherry immediately. "Between hedge and wall of barn one, by yard entrance. Three metres from truck's nearside."

97

James looked, but couldn't see him. The hedge ran right down alongside the barn wall. Cherry must have picked up a few scratches as he made his way between the two.

"Three," said Nat. "Alongside farmhouse. Gap between house and yard blocked by wooden gate. Shouldn't be any trouble. Can see rear of truck in yard."

"Four," came in John. "Approaching other side of farmhouse. Can't see anything blocking gap between house and barn two this side… … Now I see truck… … driver walking back towards rear."

"OK, guys. Hold positions," James told them.

Leaving the cover of the trees, James crouched down to approach the Lexus, not an easy feat for a man his size. His gut feeling was right. The car was empty.

He moved back into the trees to make his way past the farmyard entrance, and then emerged again to take up position on the opposite side of the entrance from Cherry. Now he could see him, crouched down in the shrubbery at the corner of the building designated barn one. James told him to sneak a look into the yard, something which was less of a risk for Cherry since his outline would be broken up by the foliage.

"Nothing, Boss… … only the truck… … can't see a soul."

John's voice broke in immediately.

"I can still see the driver, but there's two other guys now. They must have been close to the front of the farmhouse. The three of them are stood at the back of the truck."

"Confirm that," said Nat, "but I'm also getting movement in barn two… … upper floor… … Shadow moving behind those slits."

* * * * *

Vadim watched the two men come towards him. His hands felt sweaty, and he rubbed them down the side of his jeans trying not to be too obvious about it. He licked his lips and swallowed, but his mouth and throat were dry. He would be so glad when this was over.

Simonenko stopped a couple of metres short of the rear of the trailer. The Arab paused beside him, and there was a gleam of anticipation in his eyes which Vadim didn't like.

Simonenko gestured towards the door of the container.

"Open it," he said.

There was a moment's pause as Vadim turned to examine the door of the container. Then he turned back to his boss, his hands twitching helplessly.

"I can't do it," he said.

Simonenko's right hand shot out and grasped Vadim by the throat, forcing him back against the trailer.

"Do… as… you… are…told."

His voice was low, growling, menacing, and Vadim trembled. He tried to speak, but couldn't make himself understood, until Simonenko relaxed his grip on his throat.

"Bolt… … seals," Vadim croaked.

Simonenko's eyes flicked up to the container's door handles, and he swore. The handles were secured with inconspicuous, grey, plastic-coated, high-security, bolt seals, the sort which could only be removed with a bolt-cutter.

"So," Simonenko told him, "get the cutters."

Vadim's eyes widened. Simonenko's hand was at his throat again, not throttling him this time, but grasping the collar of his jacket to pull him away from the trailer.

But something else had grabbed Vadim's attention. Above Simonenko's head, on the upper floor of the farmhouse, there was an open window. Behind that window, his eyes had caught a flash of movement, prompted presumably by the altercation down below in the yard. He pulled his gaze away from the window, as he tried to work out how to make his next admission without getting thumped for it.

"I did not seal the container, so I did not know what had been used. In my truck, I only have wire-cutters, not bolt-cutters."

Simonenko stared at him as though trying to work out whether smacking him around might get him a different answer.

"My friend," interrupted the Arab smoothly. "I think I have a solution. In that barn there are tools of many sorts... ... not in the best condition perhaps, but usable. Let your man go and find what he needs."

* * * * *

"The driver's heading for the door of barn one."

James heard Nat's voice clearly through his earpiece, but before he could respond, Nat spoke again.

"Shit! ... ... Sorry, Boss... ... thought he'd spotted me. He keeps glancing this way, but it's not me... ... I think he's spotted something on the upper floor of the farmhouse, and he doesn't look happy about it."

"OK," said James. "Listen up, guys... ... I want to do this while Abby's still safe in the container. I'm not looking for a firefight but, if that's what it comes to, I don't want her caught in the middle."

He heard three affirmative responses.

"Right," he continued. "Here's what we have... ...Two in the yard, no weapons visible, waiting... ...One, maybe more, upper floor of barn two ... ...One, maybe more, upper floor of farmhouse... ... and driver now in barn one... ..."

"Correction, Boss."

It was Nat again.

"Driver's in barn one, but someone was there already and pushed open the door for him to get in."

"OK... ... driver plus at least one more in barn one... ... More of them than us, but we've got surprise, so let's do this fast... ... John, if Nat puts down covering fire on the upper floor of barn two, can you make it to the farmhouse door?"

"Sure thing, Boss. Especially now the driver's distracting whoever's in barn one."

"OK, guys... ... On my word, all go... ... Cherry and I will advance down each side of the truck... ... I'll put fire into the upper floor of the farmhouse while Cherry heads for the door

100

of barn one. If either of the guys in the yard pulls a weapon, I'll take them... ... All set?"

Three affirmatives.

"OK, guys... ... Go!"

* * * * *

Vadim swung around, a pair of ancient but serviceable bolt-cutters dangling from one hand. He'd been amazed to find them so easily, hanging from a peg on the barn wall. His delight had been short-lived.

The Arab who had let him into the barn raced to the doors as gunfire erupted in the yard outside. He took a moment to glance through the crack between the doors, trying to get some idea of what was going on, and then raised his weapon to aim at someone over by the farmhouse.

He managed to get off two shots through the partially open door before a paralysing jolt sent his MP5K hurtling from his grasp. He lunged through the door in an attempt to pick it up, which was about as stupid as he could get. A heavy boot caught him viciously in the side of the knee and, as he stumbled to the ground, the same boot stamped down hard on the fingers of his right hand just as they reached his gun. He would have cradled his broken fingers to protect them from further harm, but the boot struck again; first his head, and then his other hand. He collapsed and lay still. Cherry nudged the MP5K out of reach with his boot before bending to check his victim for other weapons. He found a Glock in a belt holster and removed it.

"I'm unarmed... ... I'm alone... ... I am only the driver."

Cherry heard the voice from inside the barn. He tucked the Glock in his belt and glanced around the yard.

James was kneeling over two men behind the truck. They were lying on the ground with their hands behind their heads. One of them had the barrel of James's H&K G36, a weapon he was definitely not licensed to possess, grinding into the back of his neck. The guy was yelling something, and Cherry assumed he was calling on his men to stand down before he got his head blown off.

Nat was still at the corner of the yard, his Sig SG550 silently sweeping the apertures in the wall of barn two. John still had to be in the farmhouse because there was no sign of him, but he'd clearly spooked whoever was upstairs because there was no fire coming down into the yard.

Crouched down, back to the wall, his eyes still sweeping the yard for any sign of trouble, Cherry said, "You in the barn... ...come out very slowly with your hands on your head."

The door creaked open just enough to permit Vadim to emerge. He came through slowly, hands on his head, apprehension showing in his eyes as he looked into the muzzle of Cherry's own MP5SF.

"On the ground," ordered Cherry. "Face down, hands behind your head."

"Now!" he yelled as Vadim was a touch slow getting down on his knees.

Before Vadim could assume the prone position, everyone's attention was caught by the sound of two shots, followed immediately by the crash of breaking glass.

Above the front door of the farmhouse, a huge window of painted glass situated on the half-landing had lit the hall and staircase. Much of the glass now lay in shattered fragments on the cobbled surface of the yard. Those who turned quickly enough were in time to see a figure tumbling arse over apex onto the cobbles. It wasn't a long drop... ... not really. As long as you were sensible enough not to land on your head.

The crunch of splitting skull was audible to everyone and, in spite of all you might have read, it sounded nothing like the cracking of an egg.

A moment later, John appeared in the window's aperture. He glanced briefly at the body below him, and then looked across the yard to James.

"Sorry, Boss," he called. "He just wouldn't play nice."

Even as he spoke, Nat emerged from the corner of the building, eyes flicking between barn two and the body on the ground. Pausing just long enough to kick a weapon out of reach of the body's outstretched fingers, Nat continued across the yard to the door of barn two.

"John," called Cherry.

"I've got them," John shouted back, aiming his MP5 at Vadim and the other guy on the ground.

Cherry raced across the yard to join Nat at the double doors of barn two. They tested the doors. There was movement in one of them, but the other held fast, presumably bolted on the inside. The two men took a breath and then Nat heaved on the free door, and Cherry rolled in through the opening. Nat followed immediately but at a different angle.

James in the yard and John at the window both listened intently, but neither took their eyes from the pair they were guarding. They held their position for the best part of half a minute before the tension eased.

"Clear," shouted Cherry, appearing a moment later at the barn door.

"Where is he?" asked James.

"Bastard slipped out the back way," Cherry told him. "Nat saw him scarpering across the field… … He's gone after him in case he's trying to get reinforcements from the boat… … There could be guys coming up from the boat anyway, if they heard the shooting."

"OK," said James. "We need to get this done and get clear before anyone else turns up."

He looked over at the farmhouse.

"John, can you get down here?"

* * * * *

All four surviving villains were kneeling on the cobbles, hands behind their heads, or in one case, broken hands dangling by his side. John and Cherry stood a couple of metres behind them, watching them carefully.

James was examining the door of the container, hoping and praying that he was right about this. He wasn't sure he could take it if they got the door open only to find a crate of drugs, or cartons of knock-off handbags.

"In the barn."

He heard the voice behind him and turned to see the driver squinting up at him.

"You need bolt cutters," the man said. "I was going to fetch... ... in the barn."

James stared at the man, and then at the bolts on the door.

"Cherry," he said.

"On it, Boss."

They might have been old and rusted, but the cutters worked just fine. The doors of the container were pulled open, and they all gazed into its cavernous interior. Row upon row of packing cases filled the space. Each was stencilled with the name of the pottery whose products they contained. Each had a shipping label stapled to the wood. James recognised the one in the bottom right corner.

In front of this array, a single crate was strapped in place, its front face only inches from the container's opening.

James heaved himself into the container and used the bolt cutters one more time to sever the padlock holding the lid of the crate shut. Slowly, almost nervously, he lifted the lid.

If anyone had a pin to drop, you'd have heard its echo all around the yard.

Then he bent and reached down into the crate. Gently, tenderly, he lifted Abby from her prison, and held her tightly to his chest, tears streaming silently, unashamedly, down his face.

"Boss!"

It was Nat, emerging from the barn, breathing hard.

"Four of them, Boss... ... coming up from the boat... ... Guy in a captain's rig with a pistol coming up the road with one other... ... two more coming over the fields."

"They armed?" asked James, still in the container.

"Apart from the captain, looks like the others are carrying AK74Ms."

Reinforcements was bad news. Reinforcements carrying current Russian military assault rifles was a serious threat.

"Boss."

It was Nat again.

"A couple of minutes at most... ... probably less... ... Two will probably try for the entrance there."

He pointed to the yard's entrance, level with the front of the truck.

"We may get one trying for the barn."

He jerked his thumb over his shoulder.

"And if they've got any sense, the last will probably go for that corner where John was."

While Nat had been speaking, James had lain Abby down on the floor of the container, and wrapped his jacket around her. Her eyes were open and she was breathing steadily, but she didn't seem to be registering anything that was happening around her.

James dropped to the cobbles and retrieved his H&K G36 from where he'd laid it on the floor of the container.

"Cherry, down that side of the truck... ... watch the entrance... ...Nat, back in the barn... ... watch for anyone trying to come through that way... ... John, back to your corner... ... These guys are dangerous, so do what you have to."

As they moved off, he levelled his weapon at the figures kneeling in front of him.

The urge to put a bullet in each one of them was almost overwhelming.

Almost.

"Give up," said the Arab. "Take the girl and go. I will call off my men and we can all live."

"What makes you think I want you to live?" James asked him.

"I think you do not know who you are dealing with," said the Arab.

"Oh, I know very well, Mr Al Kasimi," replied James. "I am dealing with scum who deserve... ... ..."

There was a three-round burst from John's MP5, and James saw him turn and give a thumbs up. Immediately afterwards, there was a shout and the sound of scuffling coming from the barn, followed by a short burst of gunfire. James expected Nat to reappear through the doorway but there was no sign of him. Nor was there any further sound from the barn.

Seeing James's eyes flick away, Simonenko reached for the ceramic knife sheathed upside-down in the small of his back. He was amazed that the cursory search had not discovered it, but they'd probably been expecting something bulky and heavy like a pistol. All he'd had to do was wait his time.

This was it.

Flicking off the retaining strap with his thumb, he pulled the weapon free and swung his arm round towards James. The four-inch blade with its razor edge would land exactly where he intended, right in the side of James's neck. The black knife had no cross-hilt as such, just a slight sculpted prominence where the blade became the handle. It was only slight, but that prominence was just enough to snag for a millisecond in the silk lining of his suit jacket.

The movement flickered at the corner of James's vision, and that millisecond was all that was needed to allow him to adjust his aim fractionally and squeeze the trigger. On full auto, his G36 could spit out twelve rounds per second, but James had it set on semi-automatic. He squeezed the trigger three times. Two five-point-five-six millimetre rounds took Simonenko in the chest. The third, because he was now falling backwards, caught him under the chin and blew off the top of his head.

The Arab skittered sideways to avoid the mess, and stopped suddenly. He could now see alongside the truck to the farmyard entrance, and what he saw gave him hope.

James saw Al Kasimi smile, and moved quickly to stand behind him so he could see what had caught the Arab's attention.

Cherry was standing in the entrance, his hands behind his head. The figure behind him had four rings on his sleeve, just above the hand that held a pistol in Cherry's side.

"What would you call it?" asked Al Kasimi, rising slowly to his feet. "Stalemate, I think... ... That is, of course, if you value the life of your friend."

James knew John was behind him, but he'd no idea where Nat was, assuming he was still OK.

Al Kasimi was brushing at his suit and looking around him for a weapon. There was none within easy reach, so he simply shrugged and said to James, "My offer is good... ... Take the child and go."

As he spoke, he glanced towards the entrance where his captain stood, with Cherry as his hostage. He urged James again.

"Put down your weapons and go... ... or I fear this will not end well for either of us."

James hesitated.

Where the hell was Nat? And what about John?

James risked a quick glance behind him to see just where John was standing and, in that moment, Al Kasimi leapt to the rear of the container and snatched up Abby from the corner where she'd been lying motionless.

James was standing three, maybe four, metres away from Al Kasimi. He could easily put some bullets into him but, because of the way the Arab was holding Abby, there was no vital spot available. And, if he didn't die outright, there were no end of things Al Kasimi could do to the little girl. Throttle her, poke her eyes out, break her neck, dash her head down on the cobbles. James could see every possibility, and he hesitated.

Knowing the guy with broken hands was no use, Al Kasimi said to Vadim, "Bring me that gun... ... over there, by the wall."

Vadim looked, and saw the MP5K which had been dropped by the guy on the cobbles beside him.

Al Kasimi shouted something which could have been Arabic, or even Greek, presumably telling his captain not to shoot the driver.

Vadim stood slowly and walked over to the wall. He picked up the weapon. He recognised it, although he was more familiar with the Fort 221, the Ukrainian army's equivalent of the Israeli TAR-21. He saw that the fire selector was in the F position for continuous fire. As he walked back to Al Kasimi, his thumb nudged the selector down to the E position for single shot. His hand was around the pistol grip, and his finger slid onto the trigger.

He walked wide of James so that he came up on Al Kasimi's left side holding the H&K out towards him. It was clear that the Arab was not sure how to do this. He needed both his hands to hold Abby as an effective shield.

"Put the gun to the girl's head," he told the driver.

Vadim did as he was told, adjusted his aim fractionally at the last minute, and pulled the trigger.

As a shower of red spray burst from the right side of Al Kasimi's head, Vadim tossed his weapon into the container and reached out to catch Abby as she fell from the Arab's lifeless arms. He staggered for a moment, regained his balance, and then held the child out to be received into the arms of her bewildered father.

* * * * *

It really went against the grain for Dougie Frazer to sit on the side-lines when the action kicked off. It had taken only a couple of minutes to convince himself that he couldn't, but he had a responsibility towards young Sting. Unfortunately, Tommy Nettles had resisted vehemently the suggestion that he should get out of the car so that Dougie alone could follow after the others. The argument had become heated. Orders had been given and ignored. Eventually a compromise had been reached. Sting could come, but he was not, under any circumstances, to put himself in danger. Dougie did not want to have to explain to his boss how he'd got his nephew killed.

They found the Merc part way down a private lane leading only to a farm and the estuary. It had been driven off the road, but the tall grass of the verge had hidden a substantial ditch. The car had lurched sideways, putting dents in the lower half of both nearside doors, crumpling the front wing and probably cracking the sump.

Sting was still gazing at it in speechless horror, when the sound of gunfire was heard coming from somewhere down the lane.

Dougie dragged Sting into the cover of the trees and the two of them advanced cautiously in the direction of the river. Progress was slow, since they had no real idea of where the gunfire had come from, or who was doing the shooting. Dougie hoped it was Montrayne and his mob, but there was no way of knowing.

After a while, they saw the Lexus parked in the lane just short of the entrance to a farm. There had been no further gunshots, causing Dougie to wonder if he should risk taking a look into the farmyard. There was no point in being here if he wasn't prepared to get his hands dirty.

Peering cautiously up and down the lane, Dougie was just about to step out of the trees when he caught sight of two figures some distance down the lane. One was dressed in some kind of uniform and appeared to be carrying a pistol. His companion was armed with what looked like a black assault rifle.

They were taking great care. The rifle guy was coming up on the verge on the far side of the lane, and looked ready to duck into the hedge at the first sign of trouble. The uniform guy was keeping close to the trees. Both were watchful, and held their weapons ready.

Then, suddenly, they weren't there anymore. The hedge and the trees had swallowed them up.

Dougie and Sting had no weapons, so this was going to be tricky. Dougie was still working on a plan when he saw movement at the front of the truck. Was it one of Montrayne's men? He didn't know them well enough to be sure. He whispered the question to Sting, who'd spent a little more time with them.

Sting nodded.

At the same moment, the uniform guy emerged from the trees in a crouch and, using the cover of the Lexus, came up behind the guy beside the truck.

It was like watching a silent movie. There was no sound as the uniform guy stuck his pistol in the back of the other, and made him drop his weapon. It was neatly done.

Dougie was torn, not on his own account, but because of Sting. He wished he'd not brought the youngster along. The presence of his young companion was making him far too cautious.

"Shit," he whispered, and then in a low voice told Sting what he wanted him to do.

Leaving Sting to carry out his orders, Dougie crept through the trees until he could see through the entrance directly into the yard. Just then there were more gunshots from somewhere in the farmyard. The guy in the captain's uniform stood still, gun firmly in the side of his hostage. He kept peering into the yard, and then down the lane, obviously unsure what to do.

Dougie's head jerked to the sound of three more shots in rapid succession, and he saw a figure in a suit scrambling on the ground at the rear of the truck. The man looked foreign. For a very brief moment, the man on the ground held his hand palm out towards the captain, as though telling him to hold his position.

With the captain's attention fully on events in the farmyard, it was time to move.

Dougie tossed a stick into the undergrowth to his left and the captain's head turned. His pistol, however, remained firmly in the side of his hostage. Dougie was ready for that, and he tossed a second, bigger, stick in the same direction. The pistol began to swing towards the trees, and a round stone roughly the size of a cricket ball hit the captain flush on the bridge of his nose.

His hostage swung around, grabbed the captain's gun hand with his own left hand, and jabbed viciously at his throat with his right. The captain was no longer in much of a position to resist, but his former captive decided to make sure. Holding onto the gun hand with both of his own, he twisted and ducked and twisted again until there was an audible crack as the shoulder dislocated.

Sting strolled past the Lexus, knees quivering only slightly, to retrieve his improvised cricket ball.

* * * * *

"I did not know," Vadim was saying as Cherry dragged his captive into the yard.

"Still one on the loose," said Cherry.

"I got him," came Nat's voice from the barn.

They turned to look as the door was kicked wide open and Nat emerged dragging two bodies by one arm each.

"Stupid sod tried to follow his mate in the back way. I dropped my gun in the scuffle so... ... Always wondered what it's like to skewer someone with a pitchfork."

There was silence then, as everyone took a moment to let it sink in that it was all over.

James was holding Abby tight to him. Her arms were round his neck, her head just under his chin, and her eyes were open.

But, apart from breathing, she didn't move and she made no sound. There was obviously skilled help needed, and it was going to take time, but at least she was safe.

James looked back at Vadim.

"You were saying... ...?"

There was immense sorrow in Vadim's eyes as he looked at Abby.

"Truly," he said. "I did not know... ... He said I was carrying bad euros... ... You know... ... bad euros? I was told... ... deliver here. I have family back in Ukraine. If I fail... ... he kill my family."

His hand reached out and lightly brushed Abby's leg.

"I have little girl... ... her age maybe... ..."

He brushed her leg again, very gently, with the back of his hand. She stirred, and her arms clasped more tightly around her father's neck.

Saturday

26th April 2003

Newton Hall Dower House – 1:05 pm

James was in the conservatory, leaning back into the cushions of his favourite settee. He was dressed in jeans, with a bulky Arran sweater over a black tee-shirt. Through closed eyelids he sensed the shifting patterns of light and shade as fluffy, white clouds moved leisurely across the blue sky. A sleepless night watching over Abby, following the stress of the previous two days, had taken its toll. His body was exhausted, but his mind wouldn't switch off, constantly reviewing every detail of the previous day.

It only needed one small thing to have been overlooked, and trouble could descend on him and his friends from a very great height.

Inspector Harvey and her team had departed late the previous evening, taking all their equipment with them. Carefully crafted statements had been given, recorded and signed, but James suspected that Janet Harvey hadn't believed a word of any of them. Of course, she had wanted to see the child returned, but he was convinced she'd also been desperate for an arrest, hoping for a conviction, which could even lead to a promotion.

Which is why he hadn't trusted her to do the job right.

It was too bad that she'd had to settle for what must to her be an anti-climax, because he knew that she would be going through all their statements, checking every single detail, and looking for inconsistencies. He knew she'd wanted to challenge their stories the previous evening, but a call from DCS Fletcher had reined her in.

Eyes still closed, James smiled. Fletcher was a good man. James wondered whether the DCS, like himself, understood that true justice and the rigorous application of the law did not always go hand in hand.

He wished he could have done more for the young man whose car he'd smashed up, but Sting had refused his offer of a brand new current model. All he wanted was the old one patched up. James smiled again. That young man was unhealthily

115

attached to his old car. Maybe it held memories like... ... first time with his girlfriend, or... ...

He heard click of the door handle and raised one weary eyelid. Seeing who had come into the room, he opened the other eye and sat up a little straighter.

"Zena," he said with the beginnings of a frown. "Who's with her now?"

"Don't worry, James. Mrs Siddons is watching her. You know how much Abby loves her."

Dr Serena Walcott came and sat at the other end of his settee. Once a fellow student with Abby's mother, Zena had gone on to develop a speciality in child psychology and, more recently, in the abuse of children and women. So successful had she been that she currently held the position of Professor of Women's Studies at Newcastle University. She had been a kind of honorary aunt to Abby ever since the child had been born. She'd been waiting at the Dower House when the helicopter had touched down the evening before.

"So, how is she?" James asked.

"Barrie Harwood's a good doctor," said Zena, referring to the clinical director of a private hospital, soon to be renamed the Aullton Foundation Hospital, a charitable trust funded indirectly by James. "But this is not really his field... ... though, having said that, we've both seen such a difference between last night and this morning that we're both of the opinion that, with a good therapist, she should come through this OK."

"Therapist?" said James, alert now and sitting up even straighter.

Zena leant forward and laid a hand on his knee. It was an intimate gesture that normally she wouldn't allow herself, but these were exceptional circumstances, and maybe... ... She pushed the thought away.

"Did you think she'd just be able to snap out of it?" she asked, looking into his eyes with a tenderness she rarely dared to show. "She won't, you know. This is going to be a long process, and she's going to need help, but she will come through it."

"So... ... what do I need to do?"

116

"Nothing, James... ... Just be her dad. That's all she needs from you right now. That and the security of people and places she knows to be safe... ... which reminds me. You might not want to try putting her in a car anytime soon. She doesn't seem to remember exactly what happened, but vehicles scare her."

Aware that her hand had lingered a bit too long on his knee, she removed it.

"Barrie's got someone in mind for working with Abby," she continued, hoping James didn't notice the slight flush that she knew had coloured her cheeks. "I don't know her myself, but he says she's ideally qualified, if she's free to take it on. He said she might want to live in, at least in the early stages, if that's OK."

James nodded, still trying to come to terms with the fact that his beautiful, vivacious daughter needed a live-in therapist. Doctor Walcott, psychologist, sensed that there might also be something else that he was trying to come to terms with.

"While we were waiting for you to come back yesterday, Mr Graham explained as much as he thought I should know about what happened. It was obvious he knew a lot more than he was telling me, especially after you phoned him from the helicopter once you were on your way home with Abby."

She paused, giving James the opportunity to fill in some details. When he remained frustratingly silent, she continued.

"All he would tell me after you phoned was that Abby was safe and that those who had taken her had been dealt with... ...That's what he said... ...dealt with... ... Oh, and he also said that it had turned out a bit messy. His word again... ... messy."

The door opened again, and Bill Siddons' head appeared around it.

"Mr Cherville-Thomas is back, sir. He's just coming up the drive."

"OK, Bill. Thanks. When he comes in, put a drink in his hand and send him through."

Siddons seemed to stiffen slightly.

"I will show him through, sir, and then I will serve him with whatever he requires."

117

James gave a wry smile as Siddons withdrew.

"He likes to do things the old way," he said. "But he seems to have got worse since Abby was taken."

"It was a great shock for him," Zena told him. "And I suspect he may find some kind of security in the... ... the formality of the old ways. Just leave him to it is my advice."

James nodded, his mind already moving on to whatever news Cherry was bringing.

"Now, quickly James, before this Mr Cherville-Whatsit comes in... ... Are you able to tell me what you did to get Abby back?"

She had heard the official version given to the police the night before but, because of what Andy had told her, she obviously hadn't believed it any more than Inspector Harvey had done.

"Sorry, Zena. I can't tell you any more than you already know."

She was hurt that he couldn't trust her, and it showed in her eyes.

"Don't you trust me, James?"

"Of course I do... ... But if I fill you in on you exactly what happened, and the police at some time ask you what I told you... ... Well, what will you say?"

She looked at him, understanding in her eyes.

"Was it very bad?" she asked.

"Bad enough," he said, "And that's as much as you're getting."

"OK," she said reluctantly. "So let me just say this. I know it matters to you what this God you believe in thinks of your actions. I don't understand it myself, but that's by the way... ... What I do understand is that your God is supposed to be a God of justice... ... Now if what happened was messy, as Mr Graham put it, or bad, as you said yourself... ... and that was what was necessary to bring Abby home safe... ... well, that seems to me like justice. Whatever happened to those people, they brought in on themselves by their own actions."

She paused again, trying to gauge his reaction, but he still gave little away.

"All right... ... all right... ... I know I shouldn't presume to speak for this God of yours, but I will dare to speak for Sarah. She was my dearest friend, and you retrieved her little girl from the most horrible fate... ... So she would have loved you for that, whatever had to be done to accomplish it... ... Oh, and she'd have been proud of you too."

What James thought of her attempt at reassurance, she didn't discover as Siddons reappeared just then to show Cherry into the room.

Zena rose and, as she did so, another thought struck her.

"I don't suppose you remembered to phone the Lord Lieutenant about the ball this evening."

She could tell by the look on James's face that the engagement had completely slipped from his mind.

"Don't worry. I'll do it now. I'm sure he'll understand the short notice. Now, I expect you'll have things to talk about that I mustn't hear, so... ... ..."

With a nod at Cherry, she left in Siddons' wake.

* * * * *

Siddons had brought sandwiches and a couple of chilled lagers to the conservatory, and James and Cherry munched as they talked.

"I didn't see the kid around," said Cherry. "Is he still here?"

James shook his head.

"Andy took him off this morning to put him on a train. He's getting our new mate Dougie to find a safe house to dump him in... ... just temporarily, while stuff gets sorted."

"I thought it was sorted... ... at least as far as he's concerned."

"Well... ... not quite," James told him.

Cherry looked at him expectantly, eyebrows raised, waiting for more details. James shrugged and gave in.

119

"Inspector Harvey interviewed us all separately in the library... ... Took most of the evening... ... When she'd finished with young Richard, he looked a bit rattled, so when I got a chance I sat him down with a cuppa to try and find out what was wrong... ... You've seen what he's like... ... Blood from stones has nothing on him... ... but I did get him to talk in the end... ... Long story, but it seems some of the inspector's questions upset him. He told me why... ... eventually... ... and the upshot is I can understand now what was making him feel so scared. For his own peace of mind, it seemed best to get him out of the way for a bit while things settle down."

"OK," said Cherry, not sufficiently interested in Richard's state of mind to press for more information. "I guess it's time I brought you up to date."

James nodded.

"Let's start with Vadim," he said. "Where is he now?"

"Holland probably," Cherry told him. "He took the truck and I followed him in the Lexus to Felixstowe... ... Those new seals seemed to pass muster... ... Anyway he had no problems at the port... ... We met up later. Dougie picked me up after he'd taken you back to the chopper and Vadim headed for the Harwich ferry."

"Do you think he made it?" asked James.

"I reckon," said Cherry. "He had his own passport, and I gave him Simonenko's. He should be able to lay a bit of a trail for Simonenko... ... make it look like he jumped the Channel... ... I left the Lexus in a side street in Harwich – open with the keys in – so it could be anywhere by now. I also gave Vadim a couple of thousand to be going on with, until we can give him the rest of what you promised."

He handed James a piece of paper torn from a notebook.

"Here's his wife's bank details in Ukraine... ... Better wait til he gets back home or she's going to get one hell of a surprise."

"He deserves it," said James. "He did exactly what *I* wanted to do... ... Now, what about the farm?"

"John & Nat had made a good job of tidying up before we got back. And that Sting's a useful bloke to have around. They'd already cleared up every bit of brass they could find... ... Anything they missed, well nobody else is going to spot it either... ... And I've had a call from Nat to say that all the weapons are safely back in the armoury at the training range."

He paused for a moment and savoured his lager.

James took a sip of his own and then asked, "What did you do with the BMW?"

"The captain said it belonged in a lockup down by the shore, ready for when Al Kasi needed it... ... so that's where we left it, all safe and secure, just like the Arab would have done if he'd sailed away."

Cherry paused then, as if unsure how James would react to the rest of his story.

"Not sure you'll like the next bit, Boss... ... but it's done now, so... ..."

"Go on," James told him.

"Before I'd got back, John had shoved the captain's shoulder back where it belonged... ... must ask him where he learnt how to do that... ... and Sting had patched up the live ones as best he could. Didn't want to get any mess in Dougie's car, so we looked around for something else. We could have used the Lexus, and there was a BMW in one of the barns, but again... ... we didn't want to risk leaving forensics. Behind the X3 though we found an old, rusted cart so we piled the bodies on that and marched the live ones down to the boat... ... There was nobody aboard so Sting and I searched it while John & Nat got the bodies and the live ones on board."

He reached into the bag he habitually carried and pulled out a memory stick.

"You might want to find a way of getting that into the hands of the Essex police."

James stared at it, thinking of yesterday morning's news report.

"It wasn't... ..." he began.

"It bloody was," said Cherry. "Date and time stamp confirm it. You can see everything that bloody Arab did to her beforehand and then they even filmed her being tossed over the side. It was the one with the broken hands that did it while Al Kasi watched... ... Now, I'm sorry about this, Boss... ... but after I'd seen that, I went straight down and put a bullet in his head, broken hands or not."

James's eyes were flinty hard.

"As Zena was just reminding me, that sounds like justice to me, Cherry. Don't sweat it."

They were both quiet for a moment after that, until Cherry remembered there was more to be told.

"We found a safe on the boat... ... Thought we were scuppered with Al Kasi being dead, but it turned out the captain knew the combination. It was stacked full of cash... ... pounds, dollars, euros and some Arab crap called din something or other. That's what gave me the idea... ... Captain was now last man standing so... ... I told him I could put a bullet in him... ... and he knew I could do it since he'd just seen me off the other one... ... or I could let him go... ...Since he seemed so good at losing people overboard, I told him to find a deep spot and do it again... ... and in return, he could keep the boat and everything that was in the safe."

"I'll bet he didn't take long thinking over that one," said James.

"Dead right. He leapt at it like a starving fox on a bunny."

"Will he do what you told him? How can you trust him?"

"I can't," said Cherry with certainty. Then he gestured towards the memory stick. "But he's going to run and hide because, if you look carefully, right in the background, he's in that video too... ... My guess is, he'll get rid of the refuse, clean up the boat, maybe change its name and then find some nice quiet place that Al Kasi never went to... ... Alaska maybe, or Brazil if he likes it hot... ... and hire himself out for charter. Or maybe he'll just chicken out, scupper the boat and keep the cash."

"Pity he's not going to get what he deserves," said James.

"Can't have everything," Cherry told him, and then thought of one last detail.

"That phone call I made, Boss… … did it work?"

James nodded.

"I told Harvey I'd had a call from the kidnapper, early afternoon sometime. If she checks the phone records – which I assume she's already done – she'll see the call is listed. She certainly didn't believe me when I told her the kidnapper had had a change of heart and just wanted to return Abby without any comeback, but there wasn't much she could do about it… …She didn't ask why I was so close to where the kidnapper is supposed to have told me to go, since she already knew I was in a chopper heading for Felixstowe."

"So all's well on that front then," said Cherry with satisfaction.

"Apparently so," James replied. "By the way, what did you do with Simonenko's phone after you'd made the call?"

"Ah, well…. …I had a bit of a brainwave there. I gave it to Vadim so he could lose it in a hotel or something once he'd crossed over to the continent… … somewhere it was likely to get handed in rather than nicked. Just to spread a bit more confusion about where Simonenko ended up."

"Does Andy pay you enough?" asked James with a smile.

"Well, you could have a word with him, Boss."

* * * * *

It was late afternoon, and James was sitting with Abby, reading one of her favourite "Famous Five" stories. He saw no harm in them, even if certain public libraries had seen fit to ban them. Abby's eyelids were drooping when Zena slipped quietly into the room. He noticed the worried look on her face as she came over and whispered in his ear so that Abby wouldn't hear.

"Siddons says the police are here again. He doesn't like it because there's an unmarked car and a patrol car with flashing lights. Sounds serious."

"Intended to impress, certainly," James replied. "Look, can you carry on reading while I go down?"

He gave her the book and leant over to give Abby a kiss on the forehead. She reached her arms up around his neck and hugged him tight. It seemed a long time before she relaxed enough to let him go.

"I'll be back soon, sweetheart," he said. "Aunt Zena's going to finish the story."

He was coming down the stairs to the front hall just as Bill Siddons opened the front door to Inspector Harvey. She was flanked by two very serious looking men in plain clothes, with two uniformed constables behind as backup.

Harvey had a self-satisfied smile on her face, almost a smirk James thought, as he walked to meet the invaders.

"Good afternoon, Inspector," said James, wondering which little, overlooked detail had got him into trouble.

"Mr Montrayne," she responded, obviously deciding that felons, even lordly ones, were not entitled to polite greetings. She thrust towards him a paper which she was holding in her right hand.

"This is an arrest warrant."

"Is it indeed?" replied James, calmly taking it from her.

Inspector Harvey's eyes swept around the hall as though looking for some clue, until a cough from one of the plain clothes behind her reminded her of her duty. She turned, gesturing to her followers.

"These gentlemen are from the National Hi-Tech Crime Unit."

She paused and, right on cue, both men produced ID which they waved briefly in James's direction.

He nodded, and his eyes immediately dropped back to the arrest warrant; in particular, to the name on the warrant.

"Where," demanded the Inspector, "can we find Richard Stephen Bancroft? I assume he hasn't left since I spoke with him yesterday evening."

"You're not serious?" James replied, his eyes now focussed on the alleged offence detailed in the warrant.

The Hi-Tech Crime people now decided that this was their show, and moved forward to demonstrate that fact.

The taller of the two seemed to have concluded that the owner of such a property as they were currently invading deserved a little respect until circumstances proved otherwise.

"I'm very sorry, sir... ... er, my lord... ...but, as you can see, we have to take Richard Bancroft into custody. Evidence recovered from a fire at a computer shop in Uttoxeter, and also from Bancroft's home, have confirmed our earlier suspicions that on thirty-first of December last year, Richard Bancroft successfully hacked into the secure network of the Ministry of Defence, and two days later attempted to hack into the Government Communications Centre at Cheltenham."

"Enterprising of him," responded James.

"And illegal... ...so, if you'll just point us in the right direction, we'll take him off your hands."

Inspector Harvey moved a step closer to James and said in a low voice, "How does it feel to know you let your little girl get kidnapped because you were determined to protect someone who's a danger to national security?"

James looked down on her from an infinitely greater height and replied calmly, "Inspector, for someone in your position, you really do talk bollocks!"

Acknowledgements

Thanks to my loving wife, Jan, who encourages my imagination and allows me the time to become immersed in my stories.

Also to Dr Ruth Fish for her advice on medical matters. Any errors in this area are the result of my not paying sufficient attention to her comments.

Thanks also to my daughters, Becci and Rachel, and to their respective partners, whose enduring interest inspires me to continue the story. To Matt, I offer my thanks and appreciation for his enthusiastic response to my stories; and to Katie, my apologies for not having found a role for her in this brief tale.

A debt is also owed to my long-time friend, Richard Ayres, who took the time to proof-read the almost-final draft of the manuscript, noting errors and inconsistencies, and offering suggestions.

Finally, I would like to thank those readers whose positive comments, inspiring insights and thoughtful suggestions will, I hope, serve to enhance future offerings in this series.

For anyone who has not yet read "Breaking Chains", here is a little taster.

Breaking Chains – The Prologue

The Lammermuir Hills, Scotland – May 2005

It felt heavy in my hand. Black and warm. Over three kilos of lethal metal. I'd never held one before that day and hoped I never would again. But right now, on that lonely veranda with its long view over the meadows to the trout stream, the power in that awesome weight was my only hope of staying alive.

The magazine was nowhere near full. I'd watched him count the bullets as he loaded it. Twenty-five shiny brass tubes. But I'd already fired several. Though I'd lost count of how many, I knew I must have some left. If their plan had worked out, it would eventually have been me looking into that black muzzle waiting for one of those shiny tubes to explode and send a bullet blasting through my skull.

But he couldn't resist a pretty face. I'd often seen his eyes ablaze with desire for my body, which had been bought and paid for so many times, and now he had his opportunity. Whatever he imagined he was going to do as he tried to force me into that bedroom, it caused him to overlook the danger of getting too close. And now it would cost him his life because I had no other way of overpowering him. He would die, and I would live.

He knelt there moaning on the wooden boards clutching at his eyes, while beyond him the grass stretched away over the stream to acres of Scottish woodland.

As I watched him, my heart pounding and my breath coming in gasps, my mind jumped back over ten years to the day this nightmare began.

To a different veranda with an equally long view, on a small island over eight thousand miles away.

To a day when I was eight years old and immortal.

129

Saint Helena Island – February 1995

The day it happened began like any other. I woke with the sunrise as usual, washed without enthusiasm, dressed quickly in my blue school skirt and white blouse, grabbed my sewing, and went out onto the veranda where I sat for maybe half an hour working on the cross-stitch design which Mum had drawn out for me. I loved setting the stitches and watching the picture grow on the fabric, but I wasn't much good at drawing. On a clear day the colours, in that early morning light, seemed so vibrant, and the silk threads resonated with a mystical vitality. I could hear Mum and Dad moving about inside but I didn't pay them much attention. While they went through their own morning routine, they usually left me alone with what they jokingly called my "morning meditations" for which I was grateful, except when I felt in need of a bit of attention. Then I'd go in search of the hugs and kisses which cemented our family together.

I loved to eat breakfast out there on the veranda. It was just wide enough for the necessary table and chairs, and continued in an unbroken run around all four sides of the house, with stout posts at the corners to support the overhanging roof. I don't really know why, but I have always loved the open air. I don't just mean the fresh, clean, scented atmosphere of the island, although that was always part of it. I just loved being outdoors, and almost every morning the view from our veranda held me enthralled until I was summoned to help set the table with shreddies or wheaties or whatever other healthy goodies the latest ship had brought out from the UK or the Cape. The trees fascinated me. They didn't grow in abundance on this side of the island, but I really treasured the ones I could see as I looked out over the plain to Prosperous Bay and the grey-blue of the South Atlantic. This was the scene which Mum had sketched for me to create with my stitches.

130

Usually, my mum and dad would come and sit with me during breakfast and we would talk about what we had planned for the day. My contribution was often quite short. There wasn't a lot I could say about school, not because I didn't enjoy it, but because I rarely knew what was going to happen until it did. My teacher had been trained in the UK, at Bristol I think, and rarely did she let slip what she had planned for us to do. She kept most of us in her class in a state of eager anticipation from one day to the next and, because she was truly skilled at what she did, we were rarely disappointed. Next to my mum, Miss Shirley Thomas was my ideal role model. She was young, mid-twenties probably, with coffee-coloured skin, dark hair and laughing brown eyes. She was attractive in both looks and personality, confident and capable, and through all the terrors that followed that morning, I never forgot her.

The small breakfast table was pushed right up against the veranda rail to allow us to sit around the other three sides. The sun was not yet high enough in the sky for us to be protected by the overhanging roof, and we could feel its warmth both directly and also reflected off the white wall of the house. I just took it for granted then but, looking back now, the peacefulness and safety of that remote place seem to belong more to a fairy tale than to reality.

It was Friday and I can remember our excitement as we talked about the British warship which had anchored in James Bay the previous afternoon. I now know that a Type 42 destroyer is not huge, as warships go, but to me she had seemed massive when I had gone down to the wharf to see her with my friends after school. Dad had met some of the sailors in Jamestown that same evening and already there was talk of a football match between the Saintes and the crew of HMS Selkirk on Saturday morning. The ship was due to sail again on Sunday, but on Saturday afternoon would be open to any who could beg, buy, or otherwise coerce a passage out to her. In the evening, there would be a party on board for invited guests. Dad was confident he and Mum would be among the select few, partly because of his job, and also because he was meeting one of the officers later on to help him out with something which Mum seemed to understand but which meant very little to me.

My dad was pretty clever. I know that because he worked for Cable and Wireless and was responsible for the project to bring TV to St. Helena Island. We were all hugely excited at the prospect and I was really proud that it was my dad who was helping to make it happen. From what I could make out, it seemed that this officer needed Dad's help to send a message to some people in the UK and he needed an immediate reply by fax. It never occurred to me at the time to wonder why the message could not be sent from his ship.

The officer's name was Gordie, which is how my dad introduced him when he came to dinner on that Friday evening. I never did know his last name. I played with my friends after school as usual, only this time it involved a certain amount of ogling of the sailors who were allowed ashore, while I waited for my mum to finish her shift at the hospital in Jamestown, the only town on the island. She now worked as a midwife on the very ward where I had been born. She loved her job in spite of the fact that she knew could never have any more children herself. She had explained it to me when I had asked about the chance of having a brother. I met her that evening about five o'clock and we walked up together from the hospital to The Briars, the headquarters of Cable and Wireless to see if Dad was ready to come home.

We found Gordie also waiting there. He and Dad had finished their business and, when he commented on how much he was growing tired of ship food, Dad had invited him to dinner. Mum was a bit concerned until Dad reassured her that he had already rung Joyce, our housekeeper, to ask her to "throw something extra in the pot". I often heard him use that phrase when he asked someone home on the spur of the moment which, I suppose, is why it sticks in my mind.

Gordie was fun. He had a full beard, jet black and neatly trimmed, not bushy. And he had smiling eyes, all crinkly at the corners. He told amusing stories as Dad drove us in his Clio Williams along the narrow, winding road that led up country from Jamestown. Dad loved that little car which was so well suited to the island's narrow roads, and was pleased when Gordie commented on how easily it pulled up the steepest of hills, even with the four of us on board. He also said nice things about our house as it came into sight, and when I showed him my favourite view, he seemed as thrilled by it as I was. He played catch with Dad and me for a few minutes on the grass in front of the house while we waited for Mum and Joyce to finish off preparing the dinner. When all was ready, we all sat down in the dining room and I remember feeling quite grown up as I took my seat and placed the carefully folded napkin on my lap. Gordie didn't talk down to me like so many adults do. I didn't contribute much to the dinner table conversation but, when I asked a question, Gordie would explain in a way that was simple and didn't make me feel as though he thought I was too young to understand.

If I'd had a list of my ten favourite adults, number ten would have been bumped off the bottom and Gordie would have come in about number nine. He might have been higher except for something strange that happened towards the end of the meal. Dad filled our wine glasses - I had a small one, a very small one - and proposed a toast. He congratulated Gordie on the new job that awaited him back in the UK. As Mum and I were saying, "Congratulations", a strange look came into Gordie's eyes. It was only there for a moment and then, before I could be sure whether it was fear or anger or just a trick of the light, his eyes were smiling again. He asked my dad how he knew about the job, and Dad told him he'd caught a glimpse of the fax as it came through that afternoon from the UK in response to Gordie's phone call. I sensed a bit of awkwardness, as though Dad was embarrassed at having seen something he wasn't supposed to, and Gordie was annoyed but didn't want to show it.

The moment passed and we all settled down to play Monopoly. It was now dark outside, the sun having set about six o'clock. We didn't have time to finish the game before Gordie said it was time for him to be getting back to the ship, so Dad said we'd better count up our assets to see who had won. Surprisingly, it was me and, as Gordie said, "Well done," I gave him a hug, partly excitement, partly goodbye. He gave me a quick hug back, and I noticed that strange look again as I pulled away from him. Mum said she'd go with Dad to drive Gordie back down to Jamestown and they could then call in at the Consulate Hotel for a drink before driving back.

Joyce stayed to keep me company - it hadn't been called "babysitting" since I was about five. We stood on the veranda and watched them drive away. I had no sense of premonition, but I remember refusing to go back inside the house before the lights of the Williams had completely disappeared.

I had just finished washing and changing for bed when we heard the explosion that signalled the end of my fairy-tale existence. At that moment my life disintegrated, and every minute of that last fateful day became forever etched in my memory.

Printed in Great Britain
by Amazon.co.uk, Ltd.,
Marston Gate.